THE OUTLAW TRAIL

Along the infamous Outlaw Trail, three parties' paths will cross — with unforeseen consequences. Former lawman Rance Toller and his companion Angie Sutter are heading south to the warmer climes of Arizona. Cole Hastings, a vicious rustler, has amassed a huge herd of stolen horses intended for sale to the US Army in Arizona. And dogging his footsteps is Chad Seevers, who not only wants his herd back, but also seeks revenge for a murder . . .

PAUL BEDFORD

THE OUTLAW TRAIL

Complete and Unabridged

LINFORD
Leicester

First published in Great Britain in 2015 by
Robert Hale Limited
London

First Linford Edition
published 2017
by arrangement with
Robert Hale
an imprint of
The Crowood Press
Wiltshire

A catalogue record for this book is available
from the British Library.

ISBN 978–1–4448–3305–8

Published by
F. A. Thorpe (Publishing)
Anstey, Leicestershire

Set by Words & Graphics Ltd.
Anstey, Leicestershire
Printed and bound in Great Britain by
T. J. International Ltd., Padstow, Cornwall

This book is printed on acid-free paper

1

That trouble was coming was blindingly obvious from the moment that Rance walked into the big trading post. Old habits die hard and so he had entered in his customary fashion: swiftly through the door and then sharply off to the side with his back to the wall. From there he could observe the room's occupants and sense the likely mood before stepping forward. On this occasion he should simply have backed out and ridden away, because one could have cut the tension with a knife.

A heavy-set individual with weather-beaten features and a greying moustache was standing by the full-length counter that doubled as a bar. He had apparently entered the establishment unarmed and now gave every sign of regretting that decision. His right hand flexed repeatedly as he eyed the assorted bar trash gathering around him.

'I thought we done warned you about drinking in here, old-timer!' This sour greeting came from an unsavoury individual with a mop of greasy black hair and bad teeth.

'I'll drink where I please and with whom I please,' retorted the big man angrily. He had a firm set to his jaw and clear, but not unkind eyes.

'Whom! Ha, that's a doozy,' sneered another man, as he nevertheless glanced nervously at his companions for support. To Rance's experienced eye, such behaviour marked him out as a back-shooter: someone who was only daring when part of a crowd.

'You must have had some real fine schooling beaten into you, back in the day,' remarked yet another. 'What say we thrash it back out of you, eh, Meeker?'

Despite his parlous situation, the man called Meeker displayed a fiery contempt for his tormentors. 'Well, I reckon there's enough of you cowardly dogs to give it a try, but I'm no walkover!' So saying and without any warning, he abruptly kicked

2

the potential back-shooter in the groin.

Even as the first blow was struck, Rance was instinctively assessing each of the antagonists. In a cool, almost detached manner, he noted exactly who carried what. An ancient army flap holster would undoubtedly hinder its owner's attempt at a fast draw. One man had a vast horse pistol tucked in his belt, which was more suited to intimidation than speed. Another carried only a Bowie knife in a belt scabbard. Lethal to be sure, in skilled hands, but when surrounded by his cronies it could be a danger to both friend and foe. Yet another sported a tied-down holster rig that suggested real pace, if not always accuracy. All of this was academic, of course, because Rance had not the slightest intention of intervening.

As the first victim screamed in high-pitched agony, the situation rapidly turned ugly. Benefiting from his momentary advantage, Meeker planted a perfectly judged right hook. Then, as his second victim fell to the floor, he decided to place his back to the counter.

Unfortunately, someone had got there ahead of him; a whiskey bottle was smashed over his unprotected head and from then on the conflict was totally one-sided.

Covered in liquor and shards of glass, the lone individual dropped to his knees, completely disorientated. It was obvious that he had no more fight left in him, but that fact only encouraged his assailants. As boots and fists rained down, blood began to flow and Meeker collapsed on to the rough-cut timber. With a hoot of delight, one of the thugs up-ended a spittoon over the defenceless man's head.

All through this, Rance remained motionless. He had witnessed such cowardly beatings before, but he told himself that it was not his fight. He and Angie were just passing through. His wisest move was to take advantage of the turmoil and silently withdraw. But then the Bowie knife came clear of its sheath. Its owner was a snake-hipped individual with the uncomfortably drawn features of a lunger.

'I reckon it's time to mark this son

of a bitch. That way he'll know to give us free range in future.' So saying, he leant forward over the prone figure. His brutalized companions huddled closer in excited anticipation.

'Goddamn it all to hell,' muttered Rance to himself. 'Why did he have to go and say that?'

Moving swiftly for a big man, he surged forward across the room, taking care to avoid the rudimentary furniture. The only person likely to spot his approach was the trader-come-barkeeper, but that individual had wisely retreated to a back room at the first sign of trouble. Coming up behind the otherwise occupied group, Rance chose not to draw his Remington revolver. Instead, he deftly snatched the Colt from the tied-down holster and then launched a tremendous kick at the lunger's exposed backside. That man's shocked yelp was immediately curtailed as he involuntarily head-butted the solid counter.

As the large knife clattered to the floor, the gun thug with the unexpectedly empty holster twisted around in surprise. His sallow features were wary and controlled and he suddenly relaxed his body, so as to present no apparent threat. There was a level of intelligence in his eyes that marked him out as quite possibly the most dangerous of the group.

Automatically taking all this into account, Rance rapidly transferred the Colt into his left hand and then slammed the barrel of that weapon into the side of the nearest skull. The unlucky recipient of that stunning blow was the owner of the ancient Colt Walker. Even as that fellow stumbled back into the bar, Rance swiftly drew his own revolver, so that he then had two weapons covering the remaining ruffians. As those that could, gazed at him in shocked surprise, he favoured them with a bleak smile that completely failed to reach his eyes.

'This place has a real friendly air to it,' he drawled. 'You ought to serve food. Then maybe you'd attract families as well.'

The lean individual with the empty

holster slowly looked Rance up and down before replying. 'Very neatly done, but you do seem to have a reckless disregard for your own safety, stranger.' His voice was low and sibilant, but everyone in the room who was still conscious heard exactly what he said and his exaggerated confidence hinted at unforeseen peril. 'Why don't you lower those shooting irons while you still can and just maybe I'll let you live ... leastways until we find out who the hell you are.'

A few yards behind Rance, a floorboard creaked. The hairs stood up on the back of his neck; someone had got the drop on him and his prospects suddenly looked grim, unless...

From over by the door, there came the unmistakeable sound of a rifle's lever action. It was followed by a heavensent and delightfully feminine voice. 'I don't normally favour back-shooting, mister,' it said somewhat incongruously. 'But if you don't drop that gun, this old Henry's going to send you straight to hell!'

There was a frustrated sigh, followed

by a short pause and then the sound of a weapon being placed on the floor. As enormous relief flowed through his body, Rance angled off to the side, ensuring that his weapons still covered the group by the bar. His keen eyes flitted to the grizzled gunhand, who now stood helplessly in the centre of the room. Murderous rage at his close call suddenly became the dominant emotion and he knew that it was time to get out of there before he started to kill people.

Pointing his right hand revolver at the newcomer, he snarled, 'Get Meeker on to his horse and you might just see the day through.' He still hadn't even glanced at his saviour, but then, of course, he didn't need to.

Meeker must have been one tough *hombre*, because even though battered and bleeding, he managed to stagger to his feet with the reluctant assistance of the grizzled thug.

'Right then,' Rance continued. 'Anyone who is still packing a weapon, place it slowly on the floor. That includes holdouts, because believe me I know where to look.'

As the men unenthusiastically complied, Rance became aware that the sharp-eyed gunhand with the tied-down rig was staring fixedly at him. That individual was nodding to himself as though he had suddenly come to a decision. 'You look like some kind of law dog to me. In fact I think I know you!'

'Well I ain't and you don't,' muttered Rance softly. 'So let's just drop it.'

'I say what gets dropped in this valley, mister, and sooner or later it's going to be you!'

'And they say women can talk,' Angie remarked sarcastically from the doorway, just prior to squeezing the Henry's trigger. The rifle bullet tore up a piece of floorboard a mere six inches in front of the gunhand's right boot. That man flinched slightly, but coolly held his position.

As a cloud of smoke drifted up to the ceiling, the young woman darted a quick glance at her companion. 'How about we get out of this place, before you get the urge to burn it down?'

Rance had to struggle mighty hard to contain a smile. To mask this, he began to back away towards the exit. His revolvers remained trained on the unhappy bunch around the counter but no one was in any itching hurry to move. As Angie swung the heavy door open, Meeker and his reluctant carer came closer.

'Are you able to ride, mister?' Rance inquired.

The older man regarded him through puffy, bloodshot eyes. He nodded slowly and then winced. 'Just get me in the saddle, son.' So saying, he shrugged off his support.

'Get back to your friends,' Rance instructed the redundant man sharply and then, as Meeker moved painfully out towards the hitching rail, added in a louder voice, 'anyone following us through this door will get shot down like a dog! As you've just seen, this lady hits what she aims at.'

The only answer to that was an icily

calm question. 'What about my side arm, mister?'

Rance shrugged dismissively. 'I guess you'll just have to come looking for it, won't you?' Then he was through the door, but just before it closed he heard the defiant retort, 'Oh, you can count on that, law dog!'

While Rance heaved Meeker up on to his horse, Angie kept her rifle aimed unwaveringly at the trading post's entrance, but was still able to take in the dilapidated sign nailed to the wall: *Welcome to Browns Park, Territory of Utah*.

Favouring Rance with a devastating smile, she remarked, 'I only leave you alone for ten minutes and all of a sudden you're a lawman again. What is it with you and trouble?'

2

'We done told him not to go into that goddamned trading post on his lonesome, but Mister Meeker can be powerful stubborn.' The doleful-looking ranch-hand well knew his boss's character and seemed greatly relieved to leave him in the care of the newcomers. 'I'll wager you folks didn't know that that place used to be called Fort Davy Crockett,' he offered as a parting comment. 'Back in the days when it was Blackfoot Indians you had to be wary of, not poxy outlaws.'

Meeker was sprawled in a sturdy rocking chair in the main room of his spacious log ranch house. Angie Sutter, formally of Devil's Lake, Dakota Territory, was bathing his various cuts and abrasions. With her attention focused fully on her patient, Rance was able to gaze long and hard at her and as usual he liked what he saw. Measuring about five and a half feet tall in her socks, her well-worn travelling clothes couldn't fully conceal a trim feminine figure. She had shoulder-length fine sandy hair, good bone structure and surprisingly good teeth. Her skin was beginning to show the wearing signs of outdoor living, but to his much older eyes that just gave her character and added to her appeal. It still amazed him that a man the wrong side of forty had actually managed to attract such an agreeable catch. And that was now compounded by the fact that she had most definitely saved his life earlier that day.

'Seen enough?' Angie casually inquired. Since Meeker had his eyes closed, it was obvious as to whom she was talking and Rance twitched slightly in surprise. Either she possessed superhuman peripheral vision or she had somehow sensed his eyes on her.

'Not if I live to be a hundred,' he responded lightly. 'Which after this morning doesn't seem very likely.'

As though on cue, the rancher's eyes snapped open and for the first time since that morning's beating, he seemed to have completely recovered his faculties. With a grateful smile, Meeker gently pushed aside her ministrations, sat upright and favoured Rance with a searching glance.

'You and this delightful young lady most definitely saved my ornery old hide today. But if those sons of bitches over at Bassetts' have anything to do with it, you may well regret it. If you take my advice, you'll help yourself to anything that I possess and hightail it out of here at first light!'

His two houseguests exchanged startled glances, but it was left to Rance to form a response. 'We were kind of hoping to rest up in this area for a spell. We've been travelling for an awful long while and we've still got plenty further to go. Besides, I don't take kindly to threats.'

As Meeker sighed, his expression took on a speculative look. 'Don't take this the wrong way, son, but are you just a weary traveller or something more?'

Rance's response was motivated by genuine curiosity. 'What would bring on a question like that? If I was just on the prod, I'd hardly bring a woman along.'

'Fair point,' replied the rancher. 'But then the nights can get cold around here and you're only human. No offence, miss,' he hastily added. Then, before Rance could answer, he continued in a far more serious tone. 'For most of the time in that snake pit, I was out of it. Those pus weasels had buffaloed me good. Yet you stood the whole pack of them off and got me out alive. That took grit and know-how. And on the way out, Spence called you a "law dog". Why would he do that?'

'He the one with the tied-down gun?'

'He was! Looks to me like it's sat in your belt now. Only he's Herb Bassett's top gunhand and he won't forget what you did. No siree.'

Rance exchanged glances with Angie and after a moment's hesitation she nodded.

Emitting a deep sigh, he came to a decision. 'I don't guess it really matters. Only I want your word that you won't blab to everybody.'

Meeker appeared mildly offended. 'You have it,' he stated firmly. 'And it counts!'

'Very well,' agreed Rance. 'Until recently, I'd carried the law in a lot of towns over a lot of years. Too many, really, but then I met Angie and suddenly decided I wanted to reach old age. We are heading south, to warmer climes. I for one have had enough of snow and cold. It was just pure coincidence that we happened by when you got into trouble.'

'But lucky for you,' Angie pointedly added, 'which maybe entitles us to your hospitality for just a little while.'

Meeker appeared genuinely upset by her inference. 'You're both welcome to stay here for as long as you care to, Miss Angie, and I never meant otherwise. Not ever. My only worry is that you will get mired in my troubles.'

Before he could elaborate, the woeful-looking ranch-hand abruptly reappeared. He was clutching a Winchester and obviously had news to impart. 'Two riders up on the ridge, Mister Meeker.'

That man groaned. 'What the hell are

they doing?'

'Just sitting their horses and watching, as usual.'

Rance raised his eyebrows quizzically. 'As usual?'

Meeker struggled stiffly to his feet and gestured for his houseguest to follow. The two men walked out of the building and on to the area of beaten earth beyond. The ranch house was situated in a vast area of open meadow, which was bisected by a wide river that flowed away for as far as the eye could see. It was quite obviously perfect country for grazing horses and cattle.

Grouped around the main building were various ancillary structures. There was a barn, a stable block and a bunkhouse, along with a large corral. The whole spread displayed every appearance of prosperity and yet to Rance's experienced eye it was obvious that all was not well. There did not appear to be enough men around to service such a large ranch. The barn roof was in need of repair and the three hands that he could see were armed to the teeth and seemed more concerned with survival than putting in a full day's work. There was an almost palpable air of tension about the place.

As was often the case, the front of the house faced south to benefit from the sun's rays. Along the full length of that side an awning had been constructed to provide a shaded area. Off to the west, a few hundred yards beyond the buildings, the ground climbed swiftly to form a ridge, which offered a perfect vantage point for anyone wishing to observe the Meeker spread. Sure enough, there were two men astride motionless horses gazing down on the property. One appeared to be holding something, so with exaggerated slowness Rance made his way over to the hitching rail where his horse was tethered. Removing a drawtube spyglass from his saddlebags, he lined it up on the unwelcome observers.

As the two men leapt into focus, he recoiled slightly before offering a brief chuckle. 'Well, well. Great minds think alike.'

Another spyglass was aimed directly at him and, since its owner already had him under surveillance, it did not flinch. That man's face was hidden by his raised hands, so Rance moved on to his companion. The gunhand, Spence's, lean features came into view. Even though conscious of being under scrutiny himself, Rance took the time to look carefully. He took in the complete absence of laughter lines around the thin mouth and the cold, almost dreamy look in the dark eyes. His companion obviously alerted him to the examination, because without blinking, those same eyes suddenly settled on him.

With a mirthless smile, Rance moved his glass diagonally down to the left. He noted that the tied-down holster was no longer empty. 'Looks like our gun thug is back in business again,' he remarked laconically. 'I think you'd better tell me what's going on around these parts.' With that, he snapped the glass shut and strode back into the ranch house.

The three of them sat round a large table, alternately eating and talking. Although cut and bruised, Meeker had not lost his appetite. 'Have you heard of the Outlaw Trail?' he asked through a mouthful of beans.

'Well obviously,' responded Rance with just a hint of impatience. 'Any man carrying the law out West knows of its existence.'

'Well I haven't,' remarked Angie curiously. 'So why don't one of you big men tell me?'

Rance's expression lightened immediately and he favoured her with a broad smile. 'Why yes, miss, I'd be mighty pleased to.' He paused for a moment to collect his thoughts and then continued. 'As the name suggests, it's an escape route that runs from Canada right on down into Mexico. It cuts through Montana, Wyoming, Utah and Arizona, which just happens to be where we are headed and why we're here. It's an established route, but of course every man on the dodge will be aware of it. There are waterholes, hide-outs, encampments and friendly ranchers to provide remounts and sanctuary.' At that point, his glance settled briefly on Meeker's battered features before he continued. 'I've even heard of hollowed-out tree trunks used for hiding messages. The reason we're travelling on part of the trail is because it gives us an easier route into Arizona. Then again, we're not outlaws, so we should really have kept clear of that damned trading post.'

'Well I'm powerful glad you didn't,' their host responded effusively. 'And since it looks like you're at least spending the night, you really ought to know my given name. It's Wesley, although everyone just calls me Wes. Unless they work for me,' he added firmly. 'And then it's Mister Meeker.'

Rance laughed. 'Well I'm Rance Toller and this is — '

'Angie Sutter,' took up his companion. Then with a trace of sadness she added, 'Formerly *Missus* Sutter, but now just plain Angie.'

Wes chose not to inquire about the reason behind that and instead shook his head. 'Nobody in their right mind would call you *plain*.'

Before she could respond, he moved on quickly. 'Anyway, that goddamned Outlaw Trail is the root of all my problems. I've built up a hell of a good spread here, because I've got the best grazing and the best access to water. That's the Green River, out yonder — Rio Verde to the Mexicans. It meanders right through my land and it's what makes everything grow. Trouble is, I'm just an honest rancher, not an outlaw, but that Herb Bassett wants to run stolen herds through this part of the country and he hankers after my place.' He paused and drew in a deep breath. 'Thing is, he ain't going to get it unless it's over my dead body, which after this morning is looking more than likely!' With that, he fell silent and pushed the remains of his food away. Suddenly, he was just not hungry.

Herb Bassett slammed a horny hand down on his substantial desk and swore loudly and gratuitously. He and the un-injured survivors from the trading post were clustered in what passed for his office. The room was actually more like a gentleman's study back East, complete with thick rugs and even a selection of books that, sadly, had never once been opened. Such an exhibition demonstrated that even out West, luxurious living was possible, subject to the possession of substantial ill-gotten gains. And the owner of the Bassett spread had plenty of those.

The others watched him in silence. They were well used to his displays of temper; he ruled operations on the ranch with an iron fist. It seemed as though he was always angry at something. Possibly, it was thought, because he had no son and heir, only two strong-willed daughters, both products of a passionate but ultimately doomed liaison with a dance hall girl. Thankfully they were away in Denver for a while, living the high life on his money.

'So, Meeker's got himself a gunhand and you let him walk all over you,' he snarled accusingly. No one responded and so his beady eyes suddenly homed in on Ray Spence. 'I hear he even took your hair trigger Colt as a keepsake. That kind of makes me wonder what I pay you for!'

The gunman's eyes flashed dangerously. The fingers of his right hand flexed as he formulated a response. Bassett was a bull-necked bear of a man, rumoured to have killed a number of victims with his bare hands. He also controlled the illicit purse strings in the Browns Park region and therefore everybody's income, but still, Ray Spence didn't eat any man's dirt.

'He got the drop on all of us because we didn't even know he was there and he had backup.'

'A woman,' retorted Bassett scornfully.

Spence stared at him implacably and refused to be deflected. 'Yeah, a woman with a Henry Rifle who knows how to shoot. And there's another thing. I don't believe he's from the wrong side of the tracks. I think we've got a tin star in the valley. He shook us down like a professional and I'd *almost* bet money that I saw him once, marshalling in some cow town. *And* he carried a Remington. That used to be the weapon of choice for the old-time lawmen.' He paused briefly before elaborating. 'Strong frame for beating on skulls.'

Bassett tacitly accepted that he couldn't browbeat Spence like he could the others and so instead gazed at his employee thoughtfully. It was undeniable that the man's comments had been comprehensive and well reasoned. And if there was a lawman in Browns Park, things could get complicated.

'All right,' he announced, coming to a decision. 'You all know I can't afford any unresolved problems. When Hastings gets down here from Wyoming or wherever the hell he is, he's going to want the run of this valley for whatever huge herd he's put together and Meeker's stonewalled me for long enough. So we need to find out just what kind of law has turned up. If he's federal, then I might need to change my plans. Killing a United States marshal is a sure way to trouble, even out here.' He paused for a moment and pensively scratched a hairy chin. 'And what if he turned out to be a Pinkerton agent? Wouldn't that be a turn-up?'

Spence shook his head scornfully. 'They're not interested in rustlers. It takes real big money to get those bastards involved.' He settled his cold eyes on his employer. 'You haven't upset somebody back East, have you?'

Bassett shook his head decisively, but his eyes held a hunted look that hadn't been there before. 'All I'm saying is that we need to be careful, so I want you on Meeker's place like ticks on a steer. If these two strangers are still there twenty-four hours from now, then you'll have to get me a prisoner.' He paused and then added ominously, 'Someone who can be *persuaded* to tell us what we're up against. Savvy?'

Wes Meeker had foregone any judgmental assumptions about their marital status, or lack of it and offered just the one room to his visitors. It was spacious and dry and contained one large bed. Illumination was provided by a large kerosene lamp.

'This sure beats bedding down under

the stars, but I'm not used to so much light,' Angie remarked coyly. 'Such comfort was *almost* worth you risking your life for this morning. Question is, what would you have us do tomorrow?'

Rance took his delectable companion in his arms and grinned down at her. 'Don't rush me. I'm still thinking about tonight.'

He gently kissed her forehead and then sighed. 'But since you mention it, I have a hankering to stay around for a while. It's fine country hereabouts and it would do us both good to rest up for a spell. I know you haven't complained, but sleeping rough has been hard on you. *And* I like Wes. It doesn't sit well, seeing him get pushed around.'

'This isn't our fight,' she chided. 'Room and board just makes it even for our saving his skin. You're not a town marshal any more and even if you were, this place would be way outside your jurisdiction.'

'Four-dollar words at this time of night. I'm impressed,' he responded lightly. Then a firmer tone came into his voice as he continued. 'Maybe I'm not packing a badge any more, but I believe that we should be able to come and go as we please.' As he spoke, he lightly fondled the nape of her neck. 'And no hard-eyed gun thug is going to tell me where I can lay my hat. I've come up against his kind all my life and I'm still here to tell the tale.' With that, he gave her a gentle slap on her bottom and stated, 'Now go see if that bed's ticky or not before I douse the light. You know how sensitive my skin is and I'm hankering after a little horizontal refreshment.'

3

'Must be close on two hundred horses. Saddle broke or not, with only two men set to guard them it's too good to pass up. Whoever runs that outfit must have rocks for brains!'

Cole Hastings sat his mount in the trees and gazed hungrily down on the isolated meadow. The early morning light provided perfect clarity with which to view his prey. At his back were six heavily armed men, but on a whim he suddenly decided that he would carry out the killings himself. It was some time since he had needed to draw his gun in anger and he was well aware that in his chosen profession he had to keep sharp.

'Be sure to keep out of sight,' he ordered. 'They won't fret overmuch if they just see one man.' Then, without a backward glance, he urged his horse out into the open.

The young ranch-hand felt alarm surge through his body as he caught sight of the lone rider. The dollar value of the herd was considerable and he had been on edge ever since the start of his watch. Although initially keen to prove his worth to Mister Seevers, the ranch owner, responsibility was now weighing heavily on his young shoulders. He glanced anxiously over at his equally youthful partner, Davy, some hundred yards away and whistled. Eager and alert, that individual spotted the stranger and immediately began to make his way across the meadow, wending his way between the grazing horses. As the distance rapidly narrowed, Davy called out to his friend, 'What do you reckon, Ben, drifter or rustler?'

His body was still tingling with unease, but Ben concentrated all his attention on the newcomer. That unknown quantity sat his horse like a typical trail-hand: comfortable slouch, unhurried pace, roll-up wedged between his lips. As far as Ben could see, the man wasn't holding a weapon or, for that matter, was even aware of their presence. As his companion joined him, he replied, 'Doesn't look like he's out for trouble.' Then he added hopefully, 'Maybe just passing through.'

And yet, as the stranger got nearer, that sense of unease intensified. Try as he might, Ben could not see his face. Too much of it was obscured by the old style Confederate slouch hat. Then his eyes shifted to the man's waist and his insides turned to mush. Just visible behind the saddlehorn was a very elaborate and unusual two-gun rig. The holster over the right hip was normal enough, but then there was also an angled one just to the left of the rider's belly button. No harmless drifter would be so well equipped.

'Christ, Davy,' he hissed. 'Just look at what he's packing.'

Desperately trying to control the shakes, Ben placed a hand on his revolver and called out in what he prayed was a firm tone. 'Just you hold it right there, mister! What business brings you down here?'

The stranger continued his relentless advance, but for the first time he raised his head and looked around in apparent surprise. 'That ain't exactly friendly of you, son. I heard tell that folks up here in Wyoming were right neighbourly.'

His mocking tone did nothing to settle Ben's nerves and now it was Davy who took over. He was the eldest of the two by a year and even had the makings of a moustache to prove it. 'There's nothing for you here, mister. Just turn that animal around and head back into the trees.'

By now the stranger was scant yards away from the two young men and, using his left hand, he finally reined in. A smile flickered across his thin lips, which completely failed to reach his eyes. 'You fellows sure are jumpy,' he drawled. 'I'm on my way to Douglas, is all. Just thought you might have some chewing tobacco that you could spare.'

Davy twitched as though someone had poked him with a sharp stick. Swiftly grabbing his revolver, he levelled it at the stranger. 'You're a damn liar, mister,' he accused shrilly. 'Douglas is back the way you've come. You'd better unfasten that fancy gunbelt and let it slide. There's death in this revolver!'

Hastings' permanently cold eyes became chips of ice as he calmly scrutinized the pointed gun. 'That's a single-action Colt, sonny boy. If you're planning to shoot me, you'd best cock it first.'

New to any kind of serious gunplay, Davy's features turned ashen as the shocking realization of his deadly mistake sank in. Even as he fumbled with the hammer, Cole Hastings drew his belly gun and with practised speed cocked, aimed and fired. As the unexpected crash startled the peacefully grazing animals, a heavy lead bullet smashed into Davy's jaw before exiting through the back of his skull in a mess of blood and brain matter.

As his long-time friend tumbled out of the saddle, Ben howled out with shock and anger and drew his own weapon. Heightened emotion gave him speed, but he hadn't even drawn a bead before the gunfighter's revolver again belched forth fire and smoke. The bullet stuck him in the left shoulder, spinning the young ranch-hand off his horse and down on to the grass. With dispassionate malice, Hastings urged his horse forward and then fired again. This time Ben was struck a hammer blow in the back. After coughing up a stream of blood, his head fell forward and he lay completely still.

As the deadly shootist surveyed his handiwork, he heard his companions gallop up behind him. 'By God, Cole,' one of them called out admiringly, 'you're a cool one and that's no error.'

Hastings favoured him with a genuine laugh. 'Yeah, I've still got the moves.' Then he glanced around at his newly acquired horseflesh. 'So now we've got even more remounts to sell to the United States Army. We can do our patriotic duty and make a shit load of money. Kind of gives you a warm glow, doesn't it? And the way those soldier boys are wearing them out chasing Apaches, means that this might be just the start.'

The prospect of future gain can be

distracting and so it was that Cole Hastings made an uncharacteristic mistake. Rather than check on his two blood-soaked victims, he merely reloaded his revolver and then led his men off to more closely inspect the ruthlessly obtained new stock. 'Let's spread out and get this money on the hoof moving, boys,' he commanded. 'We've got to link up with the rest of them and it's an awful long way to Arizona.'

One of his men, a squat ugly cuss by the name of Jake Ridgeway, responded, 'That Herb Bassett had better have plenty of good grazing for us. These animals will need fattening up some by the time we reach Browns Park and even with his men helping it's going to take time to break them all in.'

'He'll answer to me if he hasn't,' Hastings grimly remarked. 'And neither Ray Spence nor any other of his moth-eaten crew will have any say in it. The army won't pay out a nickel unless the horses are saddle-broke.'

And so, a short while later, the seven

men and their herd of stolen horses moved off in a southwesterly direction. For good measure, they had even taken along the horses complete with saddles belonging to the ill-fated guards, for use as remounts along the way. If Hastings had taken the trouble to check their back trail, he might just have noticed a spasm of movement in the grass, but he was still adrift in the euphoria that affects some men after a kill.

Sprawled helplessly on the unyielding ground, Ben groaned uncontrollably as a sea of pain washed over him. He knew that he was badly hurt, but had absolutely no idea what to do about it. All he could hope for was the welcome balm of unconsciousness. Finally, it came. But even as he drifted off, two words churned over and over in his mind: *Browns Park*. Wherever the hell that was!

Rance and Angie had slept for far longer than either of them could remember. The soft bed had seemed like a taste of forgotten luxury.

'I can't imagine why I ever let you take me away from town living,' Angie dreamily commented, as they lay there watching the morning light stream in around the heavy curtains.

'You didn't live in a town. It was a homestead next to a frozen lake and your life was just backbreaking drudgery,' he retorted swiftly. 'And the winters lasted forever, remember?'

She smiled and snuggled into him. 'And I thought it was just your charm and personality that had attracted me.'

'Well anyway,' he whispered cryptically, 'you'd better make the best of it, because it might not last.'

Angie peered quizzically over at his strong face with its full moustache, but he stared resolutely ahead, obviously unwilling to elaborate and so she gripped him all the tighter and, as instructed, made the most of the moment.

Later that morning, after an unusually lengthy breakfast, the two of them saddled up and went for a gentle ride around

Meeker's spread. Up on the ridge, one man held a solitary vigil.

'I'm surprised you haven't gone up there and had words with him,' Angie commented. 'You're not usually this tolerant.'

Rance glanced up at the high ground and then back to her. He appeared particularly thoughtful as he responded. 'Right now he's probably thinking that we're leaving for good, but he'll likely be under orders to stick around and make sure. When he sees us return, he'll have a tale to tell his boss. Then I reckon that, for one reason or another, we'll have some very unwelcome visitors tonight. So if the two of us had an ounce of sense, we'd just keep riding.'

Well slept, scrubbed and fed, Angie was looking her delightful best, but she snorted in a very unfeminine fashion. 'Only you wouldn't even consider that, because it would seem too much like running away and Rance Toller just doesn't do that.' Then she smiled broadly. 'And that's *one* of the things I like about you.'

'That must mean there's others,' he replied with a very fair attempt at smugness.

'Some bastard's going to pay dearly for this,' snarled Chad Seevers as he gazed down at the gravely injured young man. It was early evening and Ben lay on a specially erected cot in a corner of the large bunkhouse on the Bar S spread. Having lain for hours on the hard ground, with blood seeping from his broken body, it was a miracle that he had survived. The local sawbones, imperiously summoned from Douglas, had done his best. Whether that would be good enough, only time would tell. Both bullets had been removed which, on the frontier and in that year of 1881, had been a gruesomely painful process with only laudanum and whiskey available for pain relief. Small pieces of clothing had been found in the wounds and so it was the possibility of infection that was the biggest fear.

'If only we knew where they were headed with the herd,' replied Seevers' ramrod. 'Or even who pulled the trigger.

One thing's for sure, if they take those animals over rocky ground, we'll need an Indian to track them.'

As if by divine providence, Ben's eyes suddenly snapped open and he peered feverishly around the room. As his employer's presence registered with him, his lips began to move, but no sound came from them.

'Get some water, for Christ's sake,' Seevers demanded.

The grizzled doctor complied, but nevertheless issued a stark warning. 'This poor fellow has lost a powerful amount of blood. He should be left alone to rest. It's his best chance for recovery. That and youth.'

'If he's got something to say, then I want to hear it,' growled the ranch owner, but his features softened as he drew nearer to his young employee. Spots of red were visible on the fresh bandages.

This time, when Ben spoke, his words were faintly audible. 'C-C-Cole ... Browns Park... '

'Coal? What's he want us to do, build

him a fire?' spluttered the ramrod. 'He must be taken up with fever.'

'Hush up,' barked his boss. Then more softly, he remarked. 'Try again, son. I'm listening.'

'Cole Has … *Browns Park*.' His eyes were like saucers as he forced the words out. 'Shot me. So fast.'

As Ben lapsed into exhausted silence, the two men stared at each other. The ramrod, a loyal but unimaginative individual by the name of Buck Slidell, remained mystified but Seevers suddenly saw the light. 'Shit in a bucket! Cole Hastings! That's right, isn't it, son? Cole Hastings shot you and Davy.'

Ben's eyes remained closed, but he weakly nodded assent.

'And Browns Park in Utah is where he's taking my horses,' the rancher continued with great animation. 'A robbers' den if ever there was one. Goddamn it all to hell! And I left two children out there to get shot down by a gun thug like Hastings.'

'Shucks, boss,' Slidell remonstrated.

'You weren't to know there was a pack of murderers in the area. And those two boys begged to be given the chance to guard the herd.'

'Well the herd's gone and Davy's dead, but that's just the start of it. We're going down into Utah to get my property back and set things aright! Gather all the hands together, Buck. I need to put some words to them. There's likely to be some killing on this trip, so it's going to be volunteers only.'

Slidell recognized the determination on Seevers' face and sighed. 'Boss, I know you don't want to listen to this, but I've heard a lot of stories about Hastings and believe me they're all bad. He's one mean *hombre* and I reckon this could all end in tears.'

A chill front opened across Chad Seevers' features. 'Buck, nobody's saying that you have to go along. You've done more than enough for this spread over the years. Just fetch the men and leave the talking to me.'

That was just too much for the loyal

ramrod to take. Flushing bright red, he retorted, 'I never said I wasn't going, goddamn it all to hell. No sir, I never said that. And let's face it, you couldn't manage without me. *Could* you?'

Wes Meeker stared wide-eyed at the sawn-off twelve-gauge shotgun as Rance broke it to check the cartridges. To the rancher, whose main use for any firearm was merely the shooting of snakes and small critters, it appeared to be a truly fearsome weapon. 'You really think that it will come to that tonight?'

The two men were standing under the south-facing awning. Off to the west, the sun was gradually setting over the ridge, which had been conspicuously empty since the two sightseers had returned. The observer had doubtless hightailed it back to Herb Bassett to make his report. Rance looked up from his task and settled his penetrating eyes on those of his host.

'That gunhand will want his revolver back. It's so clean that it looks as though it hasn't been fired since it was proved.

Anybody who is so particular about his work is not going to accept its loss. And his boss will want to know just who you've got staying here. Tell me this: was that the first time that Bassett's men had beaten you up?'

'I think I'd have known if it had happened before,' Meeker sarcastically responded, before recollecting just whom he was talking to. 'Sorry, Rance. That just kind of slipped out. His men have heckled and threatened, but nothing else until that Ray Spence arrived. That's when most of my men left, because they wouldn't tangle with him.'

Rance nodded his understanding. 'So they've got an urgent need of your land for some crooked purposes and they're stepping up the pressure. Bassett hired a professional and now my arrival is the tipping point. He thinks you've got yourself either a gunhand or a lawman. My guess is that that son of a bitch will want to know for certain, which means he's going to come looking.'

From behind them came Angie's soft

tones. 'Is this man talk or can anyone join in?'

The rancher bowed gallantly in her direction. 'You're right welcome, ma'am. It's been a long time since I heard a female voice around here. Not since Martha died, I suppose, God rest her soul. I guess it's just pure stubbornness that's kept me here since then.'

'You'd do me a favour if you called me Angie,' responded the young woman. 'Rance and me covered some ground today; you've got a lovely spread in this valley. I reckon that's reason enough for you to want to stay here.'

Before Meeker could respond, Rance cut in. His expression was grim and his words were deadly serious. 'In which case, you're going to have to fight for it. How many hands do you have working for you?'

'Only four now,' the other man replied. 'Three sleep in the bunkhouse. Jackson lives in the main house.'

'That the miserable-looking cuss who greeted us yesterday?' Rance queried.

Receiving a smiling assent, he carried on. 'If we're going to get raided tonight, then we need everybody in one place. I think they'll go for the bunkhouse first, so get your men to move their gear into the main house and fort up.'

'Where will you be?' asked Angie warily.

Rance settled his eyes on her and answered without any hesitation. 'The bunkhouse, of course.' Then he patted the barrels of his shotgun. 'I'll have this crowd-pleaser to keep me company.'

Wes Meeker appeared visibly shocked. 'You right sure you want to do that? This really isn't your fight, whatever happened in the trading post.'

'It'll be fine,' the other man answered curtly, before abruptly walking away.

The rancher shook his head in disbelief. 'Anybody would think that I'd been rude to him. I'm real grateful and all, but he ... You two don't need to be here. It's not your fight.'

The young woman sighed as she searched for the right words. 'Rance

Toller is a good man. He's been good for me. But he was a lawman for twenty years and he told me something a while ago that I found hard to accept. He said that however you look at it, a lawman is a killer of men. There are nicer ways of saying it, but that's what it comes down to. So it means that really, Rance is just like the men you're up against, except that he does have a conscience and he doesn't like to be told when to move on. He'll do what he has to do tonight and men may get killed. If you don't want that to happen, then you'd better go and tell him, *now*!'

Wes Meeker studied her carefully as he mulled over everything that she had said. Angie was an undeniably attractive woman, but there was obviously far more to her than that. She was wise to the ways of the world and had apparently made a calculated decision to accept Rance, warts and all, when she paired up with him. It was now the rancher's turn to decide just how much he valued his spread and really there was nothing to think about.

'My younger brother, Nathan, was the Indian agent in Colorado. Two years ago, the Utes took against him and slaughtered him in cold blood. He left a wife and two children. I've promised them that they can come and live with me, but only when it's safe. So you see, I can't let myself be run out by road agents and rustlers. Whatever happens here tonight, I'm behind your man all the way!'

4

The six riders all wore clothes of muted colour, had removed the spurs from their boots and had even ensured that they were mounted on dark horses; such was their desire for secrecy. They cautiously descended the ridge and dismounted in a nearby stand of trees. The designated horse holder accepted all the reins and then watched nervously as his five companions disappeared into the gloom.

The men, with Ray Spence in the lead, all wore gunbelts, but carried no heavier weapons. Speed was valued greater than the undoubted accuracy of long guns and in any case, it was full dark and a firefight was the last thing they expected. As they neared the collection of buildings, Spence suddenly dropped into a crouch and the others followed suit. For a seemingly endless amount of time, he scrutinized the Meeker ranch. Finally satisfied that they were not being observed, he signalled the others and together they veered off towards the bunkhouse. They were under strict instructions not to tangle with the stranger, but merely to seize a prisoner.

Twenty yards away from the large wooden building, Spence again signalled a halt. The silence was broken only by the occasional sound of horses in the corral as he carefully studied their objective. Unexpectedly, there was a subdued glow coming from the only window, but he wasn't unduly concerned. The hands had quite possibly forgotten to extinguish a lamp when they turned in. Or maybe they were indulging in a late night game of cards. Either way, surprise would be total. Drawing his revolver, the gun-fighter led the others over to the entrance.

Rance Toller kneeled behind a very thick and solid overturned table. Clutching the deadly sawn-off that had served him so well in the past, he stifled a yawn and carefully shifted position. He was uncomfortable, but that was deliberate.

After some hours of waiting on events in a totally silent room, discomfort was the only thing keeping him awake. Next to him, on the bottom berth of a bunk bed, was a heavily shrouded kerosene lamp. The blanket that was wrapped around it left only the top uncovered, so as to allow the heat to escape. The resulting deep shadows endowed the bunkhouse with an eerie quality that might have been disconcerting to a less deliberate man.

It was the very faint movement of the latch that alerted him to the arrival of his uninvited guests. Although a veteran of numerous violent encounters, the hairs on the back of his neck tingled and his stomach began to churn. He knew that there was now a very real chance of the onset of brutal bloody violence.

With a slight creak, the heavy door swung open and there was a rush of men and iron. The five intruders clustered near the threshold, gazing around in disbelief. Even in the dim light it was obvious that the room was empty. But then, over by the far wall, Rance yanked away the blanket and the intervening space was suddenly bathed in light. With their eyes still adjusting from the inky blackness outside, the Bassett hands were temporarily blinded.

'Drop your guns or get to dying,' Rance bellowed harshly. Being so heavily outnumbered, he could ill afford them any leeway.

Unsurprisingly, Ray Spence was the first to recover. Leaving his men to their own devices, he dropped to the hard-packed earth floor and desperately tried to draw a bead on their obscure foe. Panic-stricken, the others began firing their weapons indiscriminately, which was to be the biggest mistake of their lives. The smoke and vivid powder flashes that accompanied the crashing detonations only served to further distort their vision. It was this collective action that forced Rance into discharging his 'two shoot' gun.

The hammers dropped in slightly staggered succession, as he traversed the weapon between shots. There was a seemingly continuous roar that battered his eardrums, whilst the cloth-covered butt rammed his shoulder with numbing power. The numerous lead balls tore indiscriminately into flesh and then the screaming started. Two men had taken the brunt of the twelve-gauge cartridges and both of them tumbled back into the log wall, seeping blood from multiple wounds.

Over in the ranch house, Wes Meeker and Angie exchanged horrified glances as they heard the fusillade of shots.

'Sweet Jesus, this is the last thing I wanted,' Wes exclaimed.

Angie, desperately fearful for Rance's safety, retorted, 'Well it's happened and we need to help him!' Turning to the ranch-hands clustered nearby, she shouted, 'Draw those guns and get out there!'

The men stared at her and then at their boss, but none showed any inclination to move. It was the mournful hand, Jackson, who eventually found the words. 'We ain't tangling with any of Bassett's *pistoleros*. We've stuck by you when others have left, but you don't pay us fighting wages and even if you did, we wouldn't go out there. We're cow-punchers, not shootists!'

The young woman glared scornfully at them, but didn't bother replying; there just wasn't the time. Clutching her Henry rifle, she switched her attention to Meeker and demanded, 'What about you?'

The rancher was made of sterner stuff than his employees. Grabbing his Winchester from a wall rack, he retorted, 'I'm with you.'

Together they burst out of the darkened building and raced towards the bunkhouse.

Panicked by the sudden carnage, Spence's remaining cronies backed off towards the door. One had a painful wound to the neck, which was bleeding profusely. Tossing aside his empty shotgun, Rance drew his Remington and aimed at one of the men. His shot was hasty and so went wide, but it completed the rout. The two men turned tail and rushed out into the night.

It was then that Spence entered the fight. Still lying on the floor, his eyes had now adjusted to the lamplight and so he finally snapped off a shot. It was more luck than judgement, but the bullet creased the side of his opponent's skull and that man flopped forward on to the overturned table and then down on to the earth floor. The smoking Remington fell from his limp hand and Rance was suddenly completely helpless.

With a snarl of triumph, the gunfighter leapt to his feet and drew a bead for the kill shot. At such range he couldn't miss and Rance's fate was apparently sealed. Then two things happened: Bassett's severe warning against killing a possible federal officer loomed large in his mind and, from beyond the door, loud gunshots sounded. Ray Spence froze with unaccustomed indecision.

Outside, Meeker and Angie instinctively split up. He pursued the fleeing men, whilst she rushed for the bunkhouse.

The rancher, whose eyes were adjusted to the darkness, got off a well-aimed shot that struck one of the fast-moving fugitives in the shoulder. That man screamed and stumbled, but just managed to keep his footing, which, as it turned out, was more than Meeker did. In his moment of triumph, he stubbed his toe on a rock and sprawled full length on to the ground.

Inside the bunkhouse, Spence had come to a conclusion. If the stranger were to accidentally die in a mysterious fire, then it wouldn't matter a damn what his profession had been. There would be no proof to connect his demise to Herb Bassett, which was all that mattered. Mind made up, he was suddenly galvanized into action.

Racing across the room, he grabbed the kerosene lamp and hurled it at the wall. As the glass shattered, oil splashed on to the dry timber and instantly ignited. Flames surged voraciously over the rough cut wood. Well satisfied with his handiwork, Spence glanced down at his defenceless victim and suddenly remembered something. Hoping to find his favoured revolver, he swiftly frisked Rance's body. Disappointment was the only result, though, as the weapon had been left in the ranch house.

Determined not to let that spoil his moment, Spence stood erect and drawled smugly, 'Well, stranger, it seems like the best man won in the end.'

Then, with the fire getting unpleasantly close, he abruptly turned away and headed for the door. Just as he reached the threshold, a slightly built figure raced out of the darkness and promptly collided with him. Under the unexpected impact, he recoiled a few paces before getting his balance. In the flickering backlight of the fire, Angie recognized the gunman from the trading post.

'Sweet Jesus, what have you done?' she cried out in horror. Desperately she swung her rifle into line, but Spence was just too quick for her. He shoved the barrel aside at the very moment that she squeezed the trigger. The muzzle flash flared brightly for an instant as the bullet slammed harmlessly into the ceiling.

'You're a feisty one, aren't you?' he barked admiringly as he crowded in on her. Before she had time to say or do anything else, he planted a sharp left hook on her jaw. Emitting a low moan, Angie dropped her rifle and would have collapsed to the floor, had her attacker not seized hold of her. Swiftly bending his knees, he heaved her bodily over his left shoulder and ducked through the door.

Outside, with his night vision temporarily lost, Spence had no option other than to proceed blindly in the direction of the waiting horses. Off to his right, Meeker bellowed out, 'Stop right there, bull turd, or I'll send you straight to hell!'

The gunfighter couldn't see the rancher, but he was more than ready for him. Without breaking stride, he responded, 'You go right ahead, old man, but make sure you don't hit this little lady. She makes a real comfy barricade.'

Meeker, now back on his feet, had no

answer to that and so could only watch with impotent dismay as Spence and his prisoner were swallowed up by the night. Then his attention was taken by another horrendous development; his bunkhouse was apparently on fire and there was the very real possibility that Rance was still in there. Sucking in a deep breath, he turned to the ranch house and hollered, 'Jackson, get your ass out here. You and the others can at least fight a fire.'

Without awaiting a response, he dashed over to his endangered building. Reaching the open door, his shocked gaze took in the blazing rear wall. Flames were already hungrily licking the ceiling and he knew in his heart that the bunkhouse could not be saved. But where was the former lawman?

With great reluctance, he entered the inferno and immediately observed the overturned table. In front of it lay both a Remington revolver and a sawn-off shotgun. It was then that he became aware of the two blood-soaked corpses sprawled on the dirt floor. Despite the soaring temperature, an unnatural chill descended on him. Regardless of his best efforts, serious blood had now been spilt, which meant that there could be no going back from his conflict with Herb Bassett.

Shielding his face against the heat, Meeker advanced to the makeshift barrier. With a sinking heart, he peered over it and discovered Rance Toller's motionless body, blood seeping from his forehead.

'Goddamn it, those murdering bastards!' he exclaimed.

With the flames spreading, the heat was becoming intolerable. He had to act fast. Snatching a glance back at the entrance, he gratefully glimpsed Jackson and his men gawping at the conflagration.

'Get in here and collect all these weapons,' he instructed. 'If the flames take them, we'll like as not all be shot.'

As they reluctantly complied, he tossed his own Winchester at the nearest of them. Then, with the help of another, he heaved the solid table around behind Rance so that it acted as a temporary barrier to the fire; that man's boots were already beginning to smoulder. Together, Meeker and his employee took hold of an arm each and unceremoniously dragged Rance out of the building. As they burst out into the mercifully cool night air, the rancher was greeted by the distant sound of pounding hoofs. The surviving raiders were making their getaway. Although having suffered a bloody reverse, they did now possess a valuable bargaining tool.

'Carry this man into the house,' he commanded. 'God willing he may yet be saved.'

One of his men emerged coughing and spluttering from the burning structure. 'What about the two cadavers in there, Mister Meeker?' he inquired after getting his breath back.

'Have you got all their possibles? Guns, cartridges, specie and the like?'

The man looked slightly sheepish at the mention of money. He had obviously hoped to keep it on the quiet and so nodded reluctantly.

'Then let the sons of bitches burn,' responded Meeker harshly. 'They chose their own fate and it saves us the trouble of burying them.'

As he backed away from the flame-engulfed bunkhouse, it occurred to him that if Rance Toller survived the night intact, then more violence was likely to be inevitable.

5

Herb Bassett rubbed a meaty hand over his big face as he inspected the battered remnants of his raiding party. His eyes took in the two empty saddles, the two wounded men and the boiling mad female sharing Ray Spence's horse. The gunfighter seemed to be enjoying both her close proximity and discomfort, but such trivia didn't cut any ice with Bassett. He was too preoccupied with struggling to understand just how everything had gone so badly wrong.

'What the hell happened?' he barked incredulously, but then before anyone had chance to answer, he really let rip. 'Anyone would think that you'd had a run in with a Ute war party, for Christ's sake. Two dead, two torn up good and only some two-bit whore to show for it. There must be easier ways to get a woman!'

That was all too much for Angie Sutter.

Incandescent rage was already burning inside her at the loss of the man she had come to love. Although her heart insisted that Rance was still alive, her head accepted that he had most probably been cremated in the flames. Elbowing Spence sharply in the ribs, she broke away from him and slipped out of the saddle. There were various men watching her with anticipation, including the lunger with the big knife from the trading post, but she ignored them all. Eyes blazing, she stalked up to Bassett.

'You sorry piece of trash. I'm no Dutch gal. I'm Mister Meeker's guest and you'll answer to the law for this night's work.'

Bassett eyed her speculatively. Mention of the law reminded him of why he had sent his hapless bunch over there in the first place. Then Spence recovered his wind.

'This was the bitch with the Henry Rifle over at the trading post. She rode with the stranger before he died in the fire.'

Bassett was non-plussed. 'What fire?'

It was Angie who answered that. 'This kill-crazy fool of yours torched Mister Meeker's bunkhouse and deliberately left Rance to die. And for what? Just so you can steal some land?' She stopped abruptly, annoyed with herself for saying too much.

'Rance who?' hissed Bassett, his annoyance and confusion suddenly forgotten. He lumbered towards her like a great bear. She could sense the power in his big frame and, in spite of her anger, took a step back. Then Spence urged his horse forward and she had nowhere to go.

'What was this man of yours?' demanded the rancher. 'Answer me or it'll go badly for you.'

'Go to hell,' came her spirited reply. 'Killing a woman is frowned upon even out here, so you'll get nothing from me.'

Bassett regarded her steadily for a few moments. There was an intensity to his gaze that frightened her, but she was determined not to reveal it. Having thoroughly scrutinized every inch of her, he suddenly turned his attention back to

Spence. 'This Rance, did you actually see him dead?'

'I shot him and then set the bunkhouse afire,' the gun-fighter replied with a hint of professional pride. 'He's toast for sure and no one can prove that you had anything to do with it.'

Bassett sighed impatiently. 'Did you see him dead?' he continued remorselessly. 'Did you find his broken, charred carcass in the ruins?'

For the second time that night, Ray Spence was plagued by confusion. 'Well *obviously* I didn't wait around to examine the ruins. Meeker was shooting at us, for God's sake!'

The big man favoured them with a half smile and nodded as though his mind was suddenly made up. As proof of that, he barked out a series of orders that showed him to be a man of considerable intelligence. 'Johnny, rustle up some help and get these two into the bunkhouse before they bleed to death. Two men paroled to Jesus is more than enough for one night.' As the young horse holder raced off to comply, Bassett turned his attention to his gunhand. 'Until I know for sure just how things stand over at Meeker's, I want this *lady* out of the way for a while. Detail two men to take her to the old cabin. They're to hold her there until they hear from me and no one lays a hand on her. Is that clear?'

Spence nodded silently, his disappointment obvious for all to see.

'Then say it!' snarled his employer.

'Clear,' responded the other man sullenly, little realizing that there was much more in store for him.

'Tell them to check the hollow tree once a day for messages,' continued Bassett. 'That way, if anyone tries to find her, there won't be a continuous trail to follow.'

Spence still hadn't given up on his attempted involvement with the attractive young woman. 'Why don't I be one of those taking her to the cabin?'

'Because I've got other work for you,' was the uncompromising reply. He had more to say, but not in front of their captive. Pointing a stubby finger at her, he remarked in a chillingly matter of fact manner, 'Move from that spot and I'll kill you, regardless of consequences. If anyone out here disapproves, they'll know where to find me!' Then, leading Spence out of earshot, the rancher continued with, 'Tomorrow morning you're going to ride over and have a parley with Wes Meeker.'

The gunfighter was aghast. 'Like hell I am. After what I did to his bunkhouse, he'll shoot me soon as look at me.'

Bassett regarded him as one might a small child. 'I know his kind. The poor fool's *decent*. If you go in alone, under a white flag, then no one will pop a cap on you. I guarantee it.'

'That's easy for you to say,' protested the gun thug, 'but it's my hide at risk and to what end?'

'Tell him there is a massive horse herd on its way from Wyoming and that we'll need his water and grazing while they're broken in. If he doesn't want this girl delivered to him in a box, then he is to cooperate. And while you're there, see what really did happen to her man friend.'

Over by the front of Bassett's impressively solid house, Angie viewed the two men with unconcealed loathing. She couldn't quite make out what they were saying and didn't really want to know. The less she knew, the less reason there was for him to permanently silence her. She just had to hold her tongue and concentrate on staying alive. That way there was always a chance that she might escape.

When Chad Seevers mounted up the following morning, he had twelve men at his back. They were already at least twenty miles from his ranch, having pushed on hard over familiar ground the night before. He would ideally have taken more men, only the name 'Cole Hastings' had put the shivers into some of his hands and in any case, he had to leave enough behind to run the spread.

After checking that every man was ready, he led the grim-faced crew off at a canter. Chad well knew that they couldn't maintain that pace for too long, but he wanted to make his intentions plain. As far as he was concerned, nobody stole from the Bar S with impunity. Not even some *pistolero* with a deadly reputation. Pursuit would be relentless and the retribution possibly bloody, depending on how it all panned out. He just wished that he had some experienced gunhands with him, rather than determined amateurs. To his knowledge, the only man with any real understanding of violence was his point man.

A short while later, as they were heading southwest towards the settlement of Medicine Bow, Chad received some unwelcome but not entirely unexpected news from that very individual. Possessing the colourful name of Charlie Peach, he had cut sign a few miles ahead. He had once been a highly regarded scout with the US Cavalry, serving under the famous Indian fighter General George Crook until he decided that he'd had enough of being shot at. Unlike most men on the frontier at that time he still

70

wore buckskins, choosing to ignore intermittent discomfort in favour of colourful tradition. Charlie was the next best thing to an Indian tracker and he had sure earned his pay that day.

'I reckon it's both bad *and* good news, Mister Seevers,' he laconically remarked. 'The pus weasels we're chasing have met up with another outfit and it's big. Hundreds of driven horses and from the depths of the hoof prints of those carrying a man, more outriders than you could shake a stick at. We must be up against well over twenty riders. They're still heading southwest and I don't believe they're just raiding at random. They know exactly where they're going.'

Seevers sat motionless in his saddle as he absorbed the intelligence. His weathered features remained impassive, but his mind was a seething morass. 'You said there was some good news,' he finally ventured hopefully.

'Yeah, I did, didn't I?' responded Charlie with a broad grin. 'The good news is they'll be easier to track. A blind man on a galloping horse could follow that trail now. That's if you still want to catch them, of course. Because if you ask me, we're a mite overmatched.'

Seevers' jaw perceptibly tightened. He drew a knife from his belt and cut himself a plug of tobacco. Just on the point of popping it into his mouth, he abruptly paused and turned to face his men. 'Who's for hightailing it back to the Bar S, for a roof over your head and regular meals?'

The question was greeted with total silence. Not even Buck, the normally voluble ramrod, could think of anything relevant to say.

'Right then,' announced Seevers with an air of grim determination. 'There'll be no turning back until we get what's ours.' He meant, 'what's *mine*,' of course, but in such a situation, he knew that it was important to grease the wheels a little.

Nodding with satisfaction, the rancher finally slid the tobacco into his mouth and led his men after the stolen herd. It had already occurred to him that if they were able to recover *all* the animals, then there would more than likely be plenty without brands and therefore no official owners. The risk to life and limb could end up being very profitable indeed!

★   ★   ★

The charred remains of the bunkhouse were still smoking as Ray Spence rode cautiously towards Meeker's ranch house. In spite of the fraught circumstances, the gunhand couldn't prevent a smile from creeping across his lean features. He had done good the previous night and the result was there for all to see.

Then the ache in his left arm reminded him that he now had the aftermath to face. His left hand tightly gripped a Winchester rifle. A soiled white shirt hung limply from the end of its twenty-four-inch barrel. Spence was grimly conscious that if that Goddamned Bassett had got it wrong about Meeker's good character, then his survival prospects were poor indeed. He was also well aware that his employer had posted a hidden observer on the ridge, so as to report back if things should go badly wrong.

'Hold it right there, you murdering bastard!'

So far so good. *He* was still alive, but apparently someone else wasn't and from his recollection that could only be the meddling stranger.

Wesley Meeker eased across the threshold of the house and veered off to the left, his Winchester aimed directly at Spence's torso. 'You've got one hell of a nerve showing yourself around these parts,' the rancher rasped. 'Give me one good reason why I shouldn't just blow you off that horse right now.'

The shootist smiled with rather more bravado than he was actually feeling. 'Because if you did that, you'd never find out what happened to the pretty lady, would you?'

The rancher's whole body tensed and yet conversely he minutely shifted his right forefinger away from the trigger.

Spence immediately caught the

movement and nodded with satisfaction. 'That's better, old man. Now you just listen good while I tell you what needs to happen. Mister Bassett is expecting the mother of all horse herds coming down from Wyoming. He's going to need free use of your land for quite a few days and, of course, your silence afterwards, if anyone should come looking.'

'Go to hell,' Meeker responded instinctively.

In spite of that retort, Spence sensed that he had the upper hand and so was completely unperturbed. 'Now there you go running off at the mouth without letting me finish. If you *don't* cooperate, the girl will die. Simple as that. Just like the son of a bitch that she came with.' He couldn't resist a suggestive snigger as he added, 'Only in her case it could take a bit longer. And don't even think about coming looking for her, because Mister Bassett's had her moved. Savvy?'

'That's a real pretty flag you're carrying, mister.' The disembodied voice came from inside the house. It sounded innocuous enough, but a dreadful chill suddenly swept through Spence's body. He recognized the voice all too well, but how could that be?

Footsteps sounded in the interior and suddenly the gaping muzzles of a sawn-off shotgun appeared in the doorway. Then the unmistakable features of a supposed dead man came into view. He had a blood-tinged bandage wrapped around his head and painful looking blisters on his face, but the awesome weapon remained rock steady in Rance's grip.

'You look like you've just seen a ghost,' that man rasped harshly. 'Only this ghost can do you some damage.'

Ray Spence's jaw worked, but no words came forth. His eyes flitted manically between the big gun and the impassive face of his nemesis.

'Where's the girl, scum belly?' Rance demanded.

The gun thug swallowed painfully as he tried to think of something meaningful to say, because in truth he had no idea where she was. He hadn't worked for

Bassett long enough to have discovered the location of the cabin.

'How should I know?' he offered dismissively. 'It's a big country. You'll never find her alone and never see her again unless you do what Bassett wants.'

Rance's eyes were like chips of ice as he followed that up. 'So it makes no difference to us or your boss whether you live or die. The man that's sure to be up on the ridge will tell him that you delivered his message and what happens next will be our reply.'

It was then that the *pistolero* realized that his demise was probably inevitable. The man before him was obviously as hardened to killing and apparently devoid of compassion as he was. Under the circumstances the next question was irrelevant, but Spence asked it anyway. He clutched at the vain hope that it might just distract his opponent. 'Just who the hell are you, mister?' he queried, as his right hand streaked towards the butt of his revolver.

The gunfighter's speed was powered by

desperation and he actually succeeded in clearing leather before the two shotgun cartridges were detonated. Rance had deliberately aimed high to spare the horse and so the murderous close quarter blast struck Ray Spence's head and shoulders. His features instantly turned to a sickening pulp of blood and gristle, so much so that Meeker turned away retching. Herb Bassett's top hand collapsed backwards off his horse and lay on the ground, a twitching mess.

'He certainly was fast,' remarked Rance conversationally. 'I wouldn't have wanted to face him down in a fair fight, that's for sure.'

Wes Meeker regarded his house guest through horrified eyes as he recalled his conversation with Angie. He was beginning to wonder if there really was much difference between Rance Toller and all those in Browns Park who sided with the outlaws.

'Who the hell is this guy?' raged Herb Bassett as he prowled restlessly around his bunkhouse. 'He slaughters my best men and I don't even know his full name.'

His ranch-hands stared at him in silence, unwilling to risk antagonizing him further. Young Johnny had brought the news of Spence's gruesome downfall and that Meeker now owned his horse. That had been enough.

The big rancher grew red in the face at the lack of any response. 'Rance the Destroyer sounds about right or maybe Rabid Rance,' he mused somewhat fancifully. 'I mean what kind of man would do that, knowing that I have his girl locked away as an ace in the hole. It doesn't make sense. He sure as hell can't be a lawman. Then again … ' he tailed off reflectively.

Bassett had encountered plenty of peace officers in his time and some of them had been kill-crazy maniacs hiding behind a badge. So maybe it was time to fight fire with fire and damn the consequences. Because one thing was for sure, if Cole Hastings and his crew of *desperados* arrived to find insufficient grazing available, all hell would break loose.

Mind made up, he searched around for the right messenger. It needed to be someone mature and not easily spooked. 'Klee, I want you to pick out two of the best horses and ride relay on them over to Robbers' Roost. Tell ... no, no that won't do at all. *Ask* Nelson Cross if he'll come back with you. Say we need his particular skills over here, fast. Make sure he realizes how many dead we've got and that one of them is Ray Spence.'

The man named Klee showed a distinct lack of enthusiasm for the task, but knew better than to decline. He was a steady 'greybeard' in his forties, who did as he was told and had a reputation for reliability. Nevertheless he couldn't resist one question before he left. 'Are you right sure about this, boss? You don't give Nelson Cross a job to do, you just turn him loose.'

Herb Bassett regarded him with barely restrained impatience. 'If you mean that the man's an animal, I know. But he's what we need round here right now, so just get moving. Savvy?'

Oh, Klee savvied all right. He took a brief look around his relieved cronies and went!

'I'm going to rest up until first light tomorrow, then I'm pulling out,' Rance announced flatly. He sat at a large table in Meeker's house, methodically pulling an oily rag through the barrels of his shotgun. Both the rancher and Jackson stared at him askance. Meeker's main feeling was surprise, but with his employee it was something more. He was tainted with the smell of fear.

'But what if Bassett's men try again?' Jackson demanded. On the face of it his question was not unreasonable. Then he forgot himself and went too far. 'You can't just up and leave us. You brought all this on. We've never had this many killings in the valley before.'

The ranch-hand paled visibly as the other man abruptly leapt to his feet and moved in close. Rance's hands were empty of any weapon, but that really didn't matter. The suddenly very nervous individual took in the livid blisters and the bloodstained bandage, the deeply etched lines and a pair of hard eyes that glittered with menace. Jackson realized that the man facing him was far more dangerous than any employee of Herb Bassett.

'You seem to forget,' Rance barked in his face, 'that this all started when your boss got himself beaten up in that piss pit of a trading post. If Angie and I hadn't stepped in, you'd have had your first killing then. Since then, I've taken a sockdolager to the head and misplaced the only person in this world that I care about. So back off while you still can!'

The last words boiled with pent up emotion that only seemed to emphasize the silence that followed. Finally Meeker cleared his throat and got between the two men. Pushing his relieved ranch-hand away, he squared up to his intimidating houseguest and held his hands out in a placatory gesture. As their eyes met, he softly said, 'You're quite correct. We mean nothing to you and he had no right to say those things.'

Meeker held his position and kept quiet until the tension had ebbed out of the situation. Only then did he continue. 'Just what are your plans?'

Rance drew in a massive breath and then slowly returned to his task at the table. 'One way or another I aim to find Angie. All I need is for you to point me towards Bassett's spread. Anyone gets in my way, I'll kill him. If it all pans out you *may* see me again. Oh and you might as well keep Spence's horse, saddle and possibles. They can go towards the cost of a new bunkhouse. After all, your man there doubtless blames me for the loss of the last one!'

6

It was around noon the following day that Angie decided to make a break for freedom. She had been held prisoner in the presumably isolated cabin for all of the previous day, having been moved there in the dead of night immediately after her encounter with Herb Bassett. That and the fact that she had been blindfolded for the whole journey meant that she had little idea of her location, but it would be worth taking a chance just to get clear of her captors. Apparently under strict instructions from their boss, they had made no attempt to molest her yet, but that was little consolation. The two men were grubby and unkempt, with hungry eyes that never seem to leave her.

Since that dreadful moment in Wes Meeker's bunkhouse, she had undergone a horrendous catalogue of emotions. They had ranged through fear, anger and heartbreak, before settling down to a numb, but ever-present sense of outrage. How dare they inflict such injustices upon her! On Bassett's orders, the man whom she had come to love and trust had been slaughtered and it was quite likely that they would eventually end up killing her so as to ensure her silence.

One way or another she had to escape, if only to gain some minor satisfaction from placing doubt in Bassett's mind regarding her whereabouts. She knew from long conversations with Rance that she would have little chance of bringing anyone to justice, because murder was commonplace out on the frontier. In addition, it was not even a federal crime and so there was no point in reporting any of it to a United States marshal.

Notwithstanding all this, Angie's survival instinct was still strong. She had ignored all her captors' suggestive taunts and questions about her slain lover's identity and silently bided her time. And then came the moment when events took a dark turn, but did at least provide her with an opportunity.

As the sun reached its zenith over the little cabin, one of the men announced his intention to ride over and check the hollow tree for messages. Wherever that was. 'Now don't you go taking liberties with this little lady while I'm gone, Billy Bob,' he warned. 'Bassett'll happily flay the skin off your feet and rub peppers into the wounds if you flout him.'

Billy Bob shivered a little at the thought of that, yet as his compadre's hoof beats receded, other considerations began to enter his head. The young lady curled up on the floor before him really was mighty pretty. And it was a powerful long time since he had enjoyed the company of a woman, unless you counted the miserable two-bit whores that periodically visited the valley. As his eyes roamed over every inch of her, a funny thing happened. His heart beat faster while at the same time, his fear of Bassett diminished.

'Get yourself over her, Angie baby,' he commanded, in what he considered to be a suitably seductive tone. 'Treat me right and who knows, I might just let you walk out of here.'

For long moments, the grieving woman did not react. She merely observed her unwanted suitor. What she saw was enough to make her want to vomit. Billy Bob had to have been excreted into the world rather than born. He possessed narrow, sloping shoulders, brown teeth, lank greasy hair and a lazy eye that gave the impression that he was permanently winking at her. What he did have, though, was a Colt revolver and a hunting knife strapped to his waist, which more than gave him the upper hand against a mere female. But there was more than one way to skin a cat...

Mind made up, Angie grudgingly re-arranged her features to form the semblance of a smile: the first one since Rance's demise. Getting lithely to her feet, she then moved slowly across the room towards the lustful outlaw. It took a long time, because at the same time as swaying her hips suggestively she was veering towards the fireplace. Her stimulating little display was having a remarkable effect. Billy Bob's eyes resembled saucers and he was suddenly sweating profusely.

'If you want me, you're going to have to work for it,' she intoned softly. 'I can't get these duds off all on my lonesome.' With that, she removed the restraining band around her fine sandy hair and then shook her mane provocatively.

The pathetic figure opposite trembled with desire and lurched towards her. Saliva had begun to trickle down one side of his mouth in a truly repellent manner. His voice trembled as he moved in close. 'Hot dang, my lovely. You're going to remember this day.'

'So are you,' she muttered ambiguously, before forcing a truly dazzling smile on to her face. 'If I was you, I'd start with my boots and then everything else will follow.'

That was almost too much for young Billy Bob. With a low moan, he dropped to his knees in front of her and began to fiddle with the laces of her left boot. It was likely to be a long job, as his hands trembled with the effects of pent-up desire. With unconcealed disgust now registering on her face, Angie reached into the fireplace.

The nights in Utah could still be chill and a goodly supply of logs had been laid in. Her right hand closed tightly around the nearest and she raised it up above her head. The unexpected movement suddenly registered with Billy Bob, but his slow mind was clogged with other matters. All her frustration and anger went into that blow as she brought the log down solidly on to his unprotected skull.

With a strangled grunt, the pathetic figure fell forward. Unfortunately, in doing so his weight fell against her legs and his arms involuntarily wrapped around them. Under that combined pressure, Angie staggered and then fell back on to the unyielding earth floor. With the wind knocked out of her, she could only lie there and gaze in horrified wonder as blood oozed from the large cut in Billy Bob's head. And then, as she desperately sucked air into her parched lungs, he quite unbelievably opened his eyes.

'You bitch!' he managed to spit out.

Tendrils of panic began to tighten around her and she kicked out wildly at his loathsome features. First one and then another blow connected and in the process Angie freed herself from those foul, encroaching arms. Scrambling to her feet, the frantic young woman raced for the door. In the process, something yanked at her left foot with such force that she nearly toppled over again. How could the poxed cur have recovered so quickly? Almost in a frenzy, she peered down.

Her relief at what she saw was almost overwhelming; in her haste to escape, she had stood on her own dangling bootlace.

'Goddamn it all to hell!' she exclaimed. 'Get a grip!'

After taking the time to laboriously fasten her lace, Angie glanced back at her erstwhile captor. He now seemed to have acquired a broken nose and lay silently in an expanding pool of blood. Steeling herself, she gingerly retraced her steps and reached down to his cutaway holster. The revolver came free in her grasp and with that she gratefully retreated to the doorway. The gunbelt and its extra shells would have been welcome, but she just hadn't the stomach to start wrestling with the unconscious or possibly even dead body.

A handgun was an unfamiliar weapon to her, but she retracted the hammer anyway and prayed that there wouldn't be anyone waiting outside. Her heart was beating like an anvil strike as the door creaked open. Beyond the threshold, the sun was shining and remarkably all appeared well with the world. Nearby, two horses were tethered to a ramshackle hitching post. Angie cursed bitterly when she realized that neither was saddled. With no idea when the other man would return, she desperately wanted to be gone from there.

Needing two hands to heave a saddle on to the nearest animal, she reluctantly lowered the hammer and tucked the Colt inside her belt. With speed driven by fear, Angie got the heavy saddle into place and fastened the girth strap. All the time, she expected Billy Bob to burst out of the cabin or his accomplice to gallop up through the trees, but amazingly nothing happened. Finally, her face coated with sweat, she was ready to leave.

With great relief, she clambered up into the saddle and took hold of the reins. The other animal eyed her curiously and on impulse the young woman decided to bring it along, at least for a while. In truth, she didn't really know whether her pathetic captor was alive or dead, but either way it made sense to leave him afoot. But where to go? Angie had no real idea where she was or where she had come from in relation to the Meeker spread. What she did understand was that she had to avoid all recent hoof prints. And so, after some frantic deliberation, she set off in a northeasterly direction: a course that would take her towards the Territory of Wyoming.

Klee (whose last name wasn't known to anyone on the Outlaw Trail) arrived in Robbers' Roost so tuckered out that he didn't give a damn about Nelson Cross's fearsome reputation. Behind him were twenty-four hours of hard riding, during which time he had alternated between two horses to conserve their dwindling strength. The tactic had worked, but it hadn't done anything to conserve his.

It was little wonder that the hideout had never been discovered by any lawmen, or at least any who had lived to tell the tale. Devoid of any genuine settlements and with no discernible trails, the whole area was a mass of canyons, dead ends and dry gulches. It occurred to the outlaw that if any area should be referred to as the 'badlands', he was in them right then. In other words it was an ideal refuge for some one on the dodge. Someone like Nelson Cross.

There were many men in and around the large clutch of ramshackle cabins, but Klee had seen the gunfighter once before, at a distance, and knew exactly what distinctive style of clothing to look for. Indifferent to the curious glances, he advanced directly into the outlaw settlement.

'I know you,' rasped the completely black-garbed individual, hunkered down in front of a fire. 'You're one of Bassett's toadies. A hired hand that thinks he's good with a gun, but couldn't hit a barn door. Come here for some lessons have you, *toady*?'

Klee regarded the man with distaste as he emphatically shook his head. 'I haven't ridden two good animals into the ground just to take shit from the likes of you. I'm here because *Mister* Bassett has need of you, which usually means there's spondulix to be made.'

Cross's eyes narrowed with displeasure as he regarded the dog-tired messenger. He was just as prone to kill a man on a whim as much as for money, but he was curious and so chose to keep a rein on his mercurial temper. What could be so important that his visitor had nearly ridden two valuable horses to death?

'If he's got trouble, why not let Spence handle it? He knows plenty about killing and that's what he's paid for.'

Klee stiffly dismounted and stretched his legs. He knew that he had the other man's attention, so why not let the black-hearted fiend wait for a few moments? Cross recognized what the other man was about and abruptly rose to his feet. In doing so he swept his frock coat back, so as to allow his right hand to gently caress the lovingly maintained Colt Navy revolver at his waist. In an era of cartridge weapons it was considered to be an out-dated piece, but one for which he had personally never found an equal. There was something about the feel and balance of it that stirred his blood, especially when he was using it.

Bassett's man hadn't reached forty plus by being stupid. Raising his hands in a display of contrition, Klee stated flatly, 'Ray Spence can't handle anything; he's dead as a wagon tyre.'

Now that *did* get Cross's interest. He cocked his head to one side, as though inviting elaboration. Klee's spine abruptly tingled as he caught sight of the gunfighter's neck. There was a thick, old scar apparently running right around it. So the stories were true, he realized. Nelson Cross *had* been brutally hung and yet miraculously survived to tell the tale.

Suddenly very nervous, words began to spill out of Klee's mouth. 'He took on the wrong man. Some fella by the name of Rance. That's all we know of him, except that he was travelling with a real pretty gal called Angie. Bassett's got her stashed at the old cabin, but he's expecting a massive herd coming down from Wyoming and wants this stranger dealt with.'

As he stopped to draw breath, Cross pointed a forefinger at him. 'This Rance. Who is he and what is he?'

'Nobody knows and the girl ain't saying. They just seemed to be passing through, but then they stayed.'

Cross peered at him incredulously. 'Some drifter you've never heard of just happens by and kills your top gun. Don't you think that's kind of strange?'

Klee just shrugged. He'd suddenly run out of words. All he really wanted was to eat and sleep, in that order.

'Well I'll tell you this,' snarled the black-clad shootist. 'The girl would have talked to me, even if it was the last thing she did on earth. But no matter. It's gonna cost Herb Bassett *mucho* greenbacks when I get involved, but then I reckon he already knows that.'

Klee eyed him warily. 'When are you thinking of leaving? Only I'm dead on my feet here.'

The corners of Cross's mouth crinkled slightly and he stepped forward as though about to sympathetically pat the messenger's shoulder. Except that by some phenomenal slight of hand he suddenly held a .36-calibre Colt. Its butt slammed across Klee's forehead and he collapsed without a sound.

'You stay here and rest a while,' Cross muttered. 'Anyone will tell you that I always ride alone.' With that, he thoroughly rifled through the unconscious man's pockets before seeking out his own horse. There were plenty of other outlaws in Robbers' Roost who had witnessed the incident, but not one would have considered intervening. There was supposedly only one code on the Outlaw Trail: do not kill. And yet unsurprisingly, the only ones who paid that any heed were either too slow or too timid. Such a bad *hombre* as Nelson Cross lived by his own twisted rules and therefore Klee was a very lucky man indeed!

Rance Toller observed the lone rider leave the Bassett ranch and some sixth sense urged him to follow. He had been waiting impatiently in a nearby stand of trees for some time. Jackson, having acted as temporary guide, had gratefully returned to his boss. It was obvious to him that Rance was a cold-blooded killer and he wanted no part of him.

By occasionally using his drawtube spyglass, Rance was able to trail the ranchhand at a distance and so avoid detection. The man was obviously jumpy, because he kept reining in to check his back trail and he rode with a cocked rifle cradled in the crook of his left arm. For his own part, Rance was armed to the teeth as usual, because old habits die hard. He had no illusions as to what he was up against in the Browns Park valley. Every man that he was likely to encounter would be outlawed up. So in addition to the Remington at his waist, he had a .32-calibre revolver in a shoulder holster as a weapon of last resort, a Winchester carbine in a saddle scabbard and the twelve-gauge shotgun hanging by a short loop from the saddlehorn. All these firearms had served him well during his long years as a town marshal in various tough cow towns.

For close to two hours, he laboriously trailed Bassett's man. Stop, start, meander one way and then another, but all the time they were heading north. Then, when Rance was beginning to think that he had been drawn off on a fool's errand, the man pulled up close to an ageing big-tooth maple tree and dismounted. It was no call of nature, either, because he reached into his pocket and drew out an oilskin packet. Bending down in front of the broad tree, he slipped the object through a large slit in the bark and then returned to his horse.

Without a backward glance, the rider immediately began to retrace his steps. Rance could almost sense his relief at what he obviously considered to be a tough job well done. Carelessly though, the man no longer scrutinized his surroundings as he rode, which could well be a sure way to sudden death. Taking a snap decision, Rance drew his Winchester from its scabbard and levered up a cartridge. Tucking the butt tightly into his shoulder, he drew a fine bead on the retreating figure. His forefinger tightened on the trigger and then, curiously, he froze.

Killing for killing's sake had never been part of his creed and he also realized that, in this instance, he would be doing himself a disservice. If the delivery boy failed to return, Herb Bassett would conclude that something was wrong and might well send out more men to investigate.

Drawing in a deep breath, the concealed sharpshooter eased down the hammer and allowed the tension to drain from his body.

Long minutes passed as Rance watched the very lucky survivor disappear from view. Only then did he urge his horse forward towards the maple. He had to admit that it was a cunning place for a message drop. The narrow slit accessed a sizeable hollow that could easily have held a dozen communications. On this occasion there was only one, but its content was illuminating and Bassett's spidery scrawl was easy to read:

THE TARNAL STRANGER STILL LIVES. SPENCE MURDERED BY HIM. HAVE SUMMONED HELP. KEEP THE GIRL AT THE CABIN AND OUT OF SIGHT UNTIL YOU HEAR FROM ME. REMEMBER, DON'T NOBODY TOUCH HER. SHE'S MY ACE IN THE HOLE. AND BE ON YOUR GUARD!

Rance stared long and hard at the grubby piece of paper. It had been quite a while since anyone had called him a murderer and it didn't sit well. As to who had been summoned, well that had to mean one or more gun thugs were heading into the valley. So he had to rescue Angie lickety split and get the hell out of there. Wes Meeker would just have to look out for himself. One way or another, the two of them had at least given him a little more time.

Carefully refolding the note and putting it back in the oilskin, he slipped it back in the hollow tree. Sooner or later, someone would come looking and then all Rance had to do was follow him back to the cabin. Moving off out of sight, he hunkered down behind some boulders, Winchester in one hand and spyglass in the other.

He didn't have long to wait. The sun had just passed its apex when along came another Bassett hand. This one displayed no particular caution and rode straight towards the tree without looking left or right. As he drew closer, Rance felt a surge of recognition. It was the grizzled gun hand that had got the drop on him in the trading post, or at least he thought he had, prior to Angie's sudden appearance. A cold smile spread across Rance's features. If that fellow was now one of the lady's jailors, then he was due for an unpleasant surprise once he returned to the cabin.

Under Rance's watchful gaze, the man dismounted right next to the tree and, unhesitatingly, reached in. He extracted the packet and then abruptly froze. For seemingly endless seconds the outlaw remained motionless. The sun cast a shadow over his features and so try as he might Rance could not catch his reaction.

'What the hell's he doing?' he pondered desperately. 'The bastard hasn't even read the note.'

Then, without any warning, the man exploded into action. In one seamless movement, he swung up into the saddle and viciously spurred his horse back the way he had come.

'Jesus Christ, a telltale,' Rance snarled with bitter realization as he retracted the hammer on the carbine. He knew with grim certainty what had to be done. If the fugitive got clean away from him, Angie would be moved elsewhere and he would be back to square one and yet, the same would be true if he killed him.

Aiming directly at the animal's haunches, the former lawman smoothly squeezed the trigger. The burst of powder smoke obscured the target, but it mattered little; Rance just didn't miss a shot like that. Chambering in another cartridge, he mounted up and sped off in pursuit. As he pounded hell for leather towards the stricken beast, he noticed its rider stagger to his feet.

'You reach for any kind of firearm, you'll end up like your horse, mister,' Rance bellowed out.

That individual swayed unsteadily and tried to focus on his approaching assailant. The fall had badly shaken him and blood poured from a gash on his left cheek. Finally, as the implacable horse-man pulled up next to him, his vision began to clear and he posed the question that seemed to be on everybody's lips. 'Just who the hell are you, law dog?'

His attacker sighed wearily. 'Like I keep telling everyone, I'm just passing through. Now unbuckle that gunbelt and pass it up here. Try anything stupid and I'll turn your head into a canoe.'

The uncompromising threat regis-tered and the man handed over the belt, but he couldn't resist a muttered aside. 'Spence'll settle you good for this, just see if he doesn't.'

Rance regarded him with grim amuse-ment. 'If you'd taken the trouble to read that note, you'd know that he's mustered out — for good.' Ignoring his prisoner's shocked expression, he added, 'And since you're going to be my guide to the cabin, I'd better know your name. Or will I have to beat it out of you?'

Any remaining fight had gone out of him at the stunning news and the grizzled gunman replied immediately. 'Tucker.

Amos Tucker.'

'Well, Amos Tucker, unless you're as stupid as you look, you'll know what I expect from you now. And if anything's happened to that lady, you'll be joining Spence in the hereafter. Savvy?'

Oh, he savvied. 'She was in wonderful health the last I saw of her, mister,' he offered desperately. 'We's both under orders not to harm her. She'll be waiting for you with open arms, you just see if she ain't!'

7

The stolen horse herd and its outriders had covered an awful lot of distance since the murderous assault on the Bar S spread. They were approaching the invisible junction of the State of Colorado and the Territories of Wyoming and Utah. That fact was probably unknown to most of the outlaws and would, in any case, have held little significance. Their criminal activities routinely involved the crossing of borders, even into the sovereign countries of Canada and Mexico.

Jake Ridgeway had been riding point; he was glad to get away from the choking dust of the massive herd. It was only when he spotted something unusual that he reluctantly headed back to report in.

'We got company, Cole. One rider leading a spare horse.'

Hastings reined in and wearily regarded the other man. Tired, dirty and irritable, it occurred to him that nobody in his outfit seemed to possess any initiative. 'So, that means he's got more than he needs and we've got less than we want. Go and explain that to him.'

'She!'

'Say what?'

'It's a female,' Jake persisted. 'I thought that would be the kind of thing you'd like to know about.'

Choosing to ignore the tame attempt at sarcasm, Hastings spurred his animal forward. It did occur to him that with his luck the woman would probably be seventy years old, with sagging skin and no teeth, but anything was worth a look to break the monotony of the journey.

Angie was beginning to feel the onset of genuine anxiety. She had been riding for hours with no sign of any pursuit, but was completely lost. She knew from the position of the sun that she was heading north, which was probably the wrong way, but then south would have taken her back towards Bassett's men. It would possibly have made sense to double back in a wide semi-circle, but she was wholly unfamiliar with the region. She had found a few strips of beef jerky in a saddle-bag, but faced with a night alone that was pitifully poor fare.

It was when she topped a small rise that Angie discovered she was no longer alone. Two widely spaced horsemen were converging on her at a trot, which meant that they had already been aware of her presence. A barrage of emotions immediately assailed her. They quite obviously weren't savage tribesmen and they would probably be carrying food, but were they friendly? They were unlikely to work for Herb Bassett, yet according to Rance the territory was infested with outlaws. Thinking of that fine man, she considered what he would have done in such a situation. Urging her horse around so that her back was to the approaching riders, she removed the revolver from her belt. Carefully cocking it, she placed it inside her jacket and then turned back to face whatever trouble might be coming her way.

As the two men got closer, her heart sank. They were both dusty and bedraggled as one would have expected, but there was something indefinably menacing about them as well. One was a squat, ugly cuss whose eyes openly devoured her, but it was the other man who made her heart beat faster. He wore a Confederate slouch hat that had seen better days and sported a fancy two-gun rig, which marked him out as some kind of gunhand. But it was his eyes that really affected her. There was a reptilian-like quality to them as they peered out from under the low hat rim and it seemed somehow natural that he would be the first to speak.

'Well, well, little lady, you *are* a sight for sore eyes. If I'd known you were in these parts, I'd have abandoned the herd and come running long ago.'

Despite her nervousness, anger began to simmer within. She was well and truly tired of being regarded as merely a sex object. 'Anybody would think I was the first woman to set foot in Utah,' she sharply retorted.

Cole Hastings laughed and casually produced the makings for a roll-up. 'That's because all the others are whores with smallpox scars and bad breath, whereas you look good enough to eat.'

At that point, Jake Ridgeway began to ease his mount towards her and Angie felt a stab of real fear as she realized that these men were quite probably far more dangerous than the two she had escaped from. If she was going to make a move, it had to be then. Without any preamble, her right hand slipped into her jacket and abruptly reappeared with the cocked revolver.

'If either of you come near me, I'll shoot!'

The 'ugly cuss' halted his horse instantly, whereas the other man merely smiled and continued to construct his smoke. 'Well, well. You *are* full of surprises,' he finally remarked. 'Attractive *and* dangerous in equal measure. So what happens now, Miss … ?'

'You haven't earned the right to know my name,' she replied spiritedly. 'And if you do not allow me to pass, then you will surely suffer for it!'

Disconcertingly, the only response to that threat was a hacking laugh from the man in the slouch hat. It wasn't until he had ignited his roll-up and taken a first puff at it that he responded. 'I don't believe that you've got the *cojones* to kill in cold blood and so I say we will not move. What do you reckon to that, Miss Spitfire?'

It was at that very instant that the vanguard of the herd came into view behind the two men and its appearance gave the increasingly desperate young woman an idea. For some moments, she agitatedly observed her persecutors as though trying to come to a decision. In reality, she was allowing the vast number of animals to get closer. Then, as though reluctantly acknowledging defeat, she slowly lowered her revolver. As a triumphant grin appeared on Jake's face, Angie squeezed the trigger.

The bullet struck the ground just in front of Hasting's horse, causing it to leap sideways in alarm. With Jake gawping at her in amazement, she cocked and fired again in front of his animal and then spurred her own horse forward. Clinging on for dear life, she charged between the pre-occupied men, all the while frantically urging the beast up to speed. Her plan was quite simple: to ride hell for leather straight through the oncoming herd and out of sight before pursuit could be organized.

Having got his own animal under control, Cole Hastings observed her frenzied departure with a grudging admiration that he wouldn't have wasted on a man. The female obviously possessed brains and guts as well as looks and his preference was for her to inhabit his bedroll rather than a cold hole in the ground. It was this fact that influenced his aim as he levelled a revolver at the fast receding target. She had nearly reached the herd, so he had little time. That additional pressure, when sighting on her horse, also minutely affected the shot. Even as he fired, the gunfighter knew that he had messed up. The bullet took Angie's horse in its right flank. It whinnied with pain, but maintained a gallop and suddenly they were in amongst the herd. For Hastings, another consideration now came into play.

'No more shooting,' he bellowed at the startled outriders. 'You'll spook the herd!'

In amongst the vast sea of horseflesh, Angie eased back on the reins. There was no point risking a collision and she needed to conserve her animal's strength. The beast was wounded, but apparently not mortally so ... yet!

Hastings left Jake to round up the woman's spare mount and raced up to his nearest trail-hand. 'Pass the word. I want that bitch caught and I want her alive.' As an afterthought, he added, 'With no bits blown off her. Now move!'

The man raced off to comply, but the problem was that no one could spot her in the midst of the seething mass of horseflesh. She had the sense to double over in the saddle and remain low.

Gradually she made her way through the relentlessly advancing herd. The noise and dust meant that she had no idea where any of the outriders were and so when she finally broke through the rear, it was pure bad luck that had her ride straight into one.

The wide-eyed trail-hand was all too aware of his boss's instructions and so kept his weapon holstered and merely made a grab for her. Angie was no hardened killer, but she had no intention of submitting. Instinctively she raised her revolver and shot the man in his right thigh. With a howl of agony, he clapped his hand to the wound and lost all interest in the crazy female. With three shots remaining, she dug her heels in and took off at a gallop. Her animal was suffering, but she was lighter than any man and they rapidly made ground. Some of the men had not even been told of her presence and so simply watched curiously as she sped away.

Cole Hastings accepted the news of her escape with bad grace. 'Son of a bitch,' he stormed. 'I really wanted that woman!' The outlaw leader was sorely tempted to go after her, but knew that it just wasn't practical. The dollar potential of the herd was huge and he couldn't afford to jeopardize that by chasing some fast trick all over God's creation.

Jake had little sympathy, because he knew full well that he wouldn't have got a look in anyway. 'Well at least we've got ourselves another horse, boss, and guess what?'

Cole Hastings regarded him balefully, so he pressed on fast. 'This one's got Herb Bassett's brand on it. That makes her a horse thief, just like us. You should have offered her a job and then she wouldn't have hightailed it like that. Ha ha!'

Hastings' response to that was thankfully drowned out by the din of the advancing herd's pounding hoofs. The thwarted gunfighter moodily mounted his horse. On a whim, he suddenly decided that he wanted to sleep undercover for a change. He recalled that there was a cabin to the southwest, sometimes used as a refuge by outlaws on the run. It would require little deviation from their route to reach it. If anyone should happen to be occupying it, then God help them because Cole Hastings did not intend to be thwarted again.

Even though he understood the reason behind it, Rance Toller was heartily sick of Amos Tucker's whining. Enforced walking came particularly hard to cowboys and the like. They would take any measures to avoid it, but Amos's options had all died with his horse. Threatened with the deliberate infliction of a minor gunshot wound, he had been faced with no choice other than to lead his captor back to the isolated cabin. Rance burned with impatience to get there, but wasn't prepared to take the risk of allowing the Bassett hand to ride double. Accordingly it was late in the afternoon before the two men arrived at Angie's temporary prison.

Highlighted with shafts of light from the declining sun, the log cabin appeared a picture of tranquillity and yet it was immediately obvious that something wasn't right. He glanced at Amos and knew that he too had spotted it. The door was partially open and there were no horses at the hitching rail. The permanently simmering anger that Rance had felt since Angie's capture began to increase its hold. When he spoke, his words were unmistakeably chill.

'You walked here because I set you afoot, but I doubt that Angie and your partner did.' The other man made no comment, so he added, 'Stay where I can see you and remember, this scattergun makes an awful mess of a man, as your *amigo* Spence discovered.'

Very cautiously, Rance circled the cabin. The only window was on the same side as the entrance and was unglazed. The shutters hung open, allowing light to enter the structure. He longed to rush in and encounter Angie's smiling face, but something told him that such an ideal just wasn't on the cards. Instead he acted with studied deliberation. Dismounting, he ground-tethered his horse and closed in on the footsore cowboy.

'What's your partner called?' he demanded quietly. His lips twisted into a cold smile as he then digested the other man's response. 'Billy Bob!' he rasped. 'Well ain't that cute?'

Placing himself directly behind his prisoner, Rance called out. 'Show yourself, Billy Bob, or it'll go badly for your limping friend here. He's already had a horse shot from under him!'

There was no response to that, which left him with only one option. 'Looks like he doesn't value your hide over much, Amos.' He angled to the right, so as to be clear of the gaping window and then rammed the shotgun muzzles into the small of Amos's back. 'Start praying and move!'

'Jesus Christ, Billy Bob,' Amos blurted out. 'Don't shoot. This son of a bitch means business!'

The pressure from the heavy gun was relentless. The helpless outlaw's body weight shoved the door aside and he half fell into the cabin. With his heart pounding fit to burst, Rance leapt in behind him and rapidly swivelled his weapon from side to side. The single room was completely bereft of life. The great surge of relief was rapidly followed by overwhelming disappointment; he had been hoping against hope to find Angie alive and well. As night follows day, the next emotion was raging anger and there was only one person available to vent that on.

Amos Tucker was not the smartest kid on the block, but he sensed what was coming and chose to strike first. Hurling himself at Rance's unguarded flank, he knocked the shotgun aside and swung his right fist. The haymaker struck his captor on the jaw and sent him crashing to the floor. At that point Amos had two choices: run for the horse or go for the kill. The burst of violence coupled with bitterness over the loss of his horse meant that his blood was up and he chose the latter. Savagely booting Rance in the ribs, he then leant over and tore the sawn-off from a suddenly enfeebled grip.

Every part of his body seemed to be in pain, but somehow Rance managed to focus on the vengeful enemy looming above him. Even as the deadly sawn-off swung down towards him, he kicked out at Amos's ankles. The desperate blow struck home and that man staggered back, his aim abruptly spoiled. Rance knew that he had one chance only. Dragging his Remington from its holster, he cocked, aimed and fired in one apparently seamless movement.

In the enclosed space, the detonation seemed shattering, but it was nothing compared with what followed. The heavy bullet caught Amos squarely in the chest and the resulting agony caused his fingers to tighten on the twin triggers. Both barrels of the scattergun exploded into the ceiling, bringing a shower of earth and splinters down into the room. The noise was totally deafening and Rance's ears rang with pain.

Amos Tucker was beyond any such sensation. His life had been snuffed out, although his demise went unnoticed due to the amount of sulphurous smoke in the cabin. As for Rance — well, his victory felt very hollow. He had no idea where Angie and Billy Bob had got to and that fact made his heart ache with anxiety. He was also exceptionally tired, a condition that had been accentuated by the sudden outburst of violence. It hit his legs first and unexpectedly he found himself remaining on the floor with no inclination to move. Slowly and irrevocably his eyes began to close.

As it turned out, Billy Bob had pursued a very strange course indeed. With both a fractured skull and a broken nose, his grip on reality had drifted. Rather than simply waiting for his partner to return, he had stumbled off in Angie's wake, correctly reasoning that she would flee in the direction opposite to that of his boss's ranch. The likelihood of his catching her was non-existent, but it did mean that he would encounter the vast horse herd on its continued way southwest and before it reached the cabin.

'What is it now?' snapped Cole Hastings testily. 'Another stray female on a stolen horse? Maybe this one's dragging a Gatling gun along to really give us hell.'

The trail-hand viewed him warily. In such a mood, he could be unpredictable, with occasionally lethal results. 'We got us some pilgrim on foot, boss. Covered in blood and snot and jawing about some woman on the run.'

Hastings blinked rapidly as he put two and two together. 'And we just happen to have a spare saddle horse, don't we? Go fetch it and follow me.' So saying, he spurred off around the outskirts of the herd.

The pitiful specimen stood motionless in open country. In truth he had reached the end of his tether. He had so much blood coating his face that he was almost blind. As the horse came pounding up to him, he didn't really care whether it was friend or foe, which was a good thing, since Cole Hastings was nobody's buddy.

'You look in a real bad way, mister,' barked the hazy figure above him. 'You must have really upset someone.'

Billy Bob gratefully sank to the ground and hesitantly told of his employer and the runaway female. Not yet knowing whom he was addressing, he didn't mention his part in holding her prisoner.

'Lucky for you we found you,' responded the outlaw leader without any noticeable sympathy. 'Since you work for Bassett, I guess we'll take you along. Who knows, you might even recognize your own horse. Think on this, though; we ain't carrying passengers. If you fall behind, we'll leave you for the buzzards. We're stopping at an old cabin for the night. If you're still alive by then, I'll let my men give you some doctoring. That all sounds pretty fair to me.'

Billy Bob nodded silently. Every part of his body was crying out for relief, but even so he couldn't help wondering whether there might be more than one cabin in the vicinity.

The horse gave out a great gasp and abruptly fell sideways. Angie threw herself from the saddle and only narrowly avoided being crushed by its great weight. Badly shaken, it was a few moments before she felt able to get to her feet. Blood was pouring from the animal's flank and it was obviously in great pain. She tried to harden her heart, but try as she may she couldn't just walk off and leave it. Common sense dictated the avoidance of a gunshot, but the prospect of slitting its throat with her small belt knife was just too upsetting. The thought crossed her mind that Rance would have had no such qualms, but the sense of loss that followed that only made her feel even worse.

Slowly cocking her stolen revolver, she pointed it at the pathetically twitching head, closed her eyes and squeezed the trigger. There was a loud crash and she felt specks of blood splatter on to her cheek. Reluctantly, Angie inspected the body. The legs convulsed slightly, but there was no longer any doubt about its condition. With a great sigh of regret, she gratefully looked away so as to scrutinize the surrounding terrain. What she saw caused her to freeze in sheer horror, the unfortunate beast abruptly forgotten.

Barely two hundred yards away, across a stretch of lush grassland, sat a single horseman. He was so still that he could have been posing for a painting, except that his eyes appeared to be fixed on her. 'Oh my God,' she thought. 'Not again!' Only this time it would be different, because she no longer possessed a horse.

Suddenly the solitary spectator urged his animal forward. Angie knew that there was no point in running. All she could do was stand and fight … with just the two cartridges that she had left. Again she cocked the Colt, but kept it pointing at the earth to avoid deliberately antagonizing the stranger. As he got closer, she realized with a start that he was clad entirely in buckskin.

'What the hell is he?' she pondered. 'A mountain man?'

Deciding against being merely a placid onlooker, she yelled out, 'That's close enough, mister. You don't look like a road agent, but I've had my fill of trouble today.'

He pulled up sharply and regarded her calmly for a few moments, before raising his hands high. 'You've got nothing to fear from me, ma'am,' Charlie Peach replied. 'I'm riding point for a rancher, name of Chad Seevers. He's got a posse of men chasing down a herd of stolen horses. From the look of you, I'm thinking that maybe you've already encountered those sons of bitches.'

Even as he spoke, a group of horsemen came into view behind him. Twisting in the saddle, he signalled for them to halt and then twisted back to face her.

'Mister Seevers might look like one tough *hombre*,' he continued, 'but he's a gentleman at heart. He'll be right pleased to hear your story and share some vittles with you.' The scout briefly paused, before adding, 'What do you say to that, ma'am?'

Angie looked at him closely and then at the men behind him. Some sixth sense told her to trust him. Besides, there were enough of them out there to ride her into the earth if they so chose. With a sigh, she carefully lowered the hammer and called back, 'My name is Angie and I reckon I'll be right pleased to meet your Mister Seevers.'

8

Rance woke with a start. To have fallen asleep in such a situation was unforgivable. It highlighted the fact that he hadn't yet fully recovered from the vicious encounter in Meeker's bunkhouse. Blearily looking around him, he recognized that darkness had fallen, which in itself presented him with a problem. He was desperate to continue his search for Angie, but he had no idea where she could have got to and it would be just plain stupid to go wandering off in the dark.

There was just enough light coming through the window for him to make out the lifeless body of Amos Tucker. It occurred to him that if he intended spending much more time in the cabin, then it would behove him to drag the corpse outside before it started to turn. With that thought in mind, he clambered to his feet and began to carefully pick his way across the room. It was then that he first heard the sound of horses approaching. They were still some distance away, but he could tell that there were a goodly number of them and they were moving at a steady pace, as though well used to travelling at night.

In such circumstances many men would have panicked, but Rance Toller possessed a steely quality that enabled him to remain in control at all times, in spite of the uneasy assumptions that were forming in his mind. Now fully awake, he abandoned any interest in the cadaver and instead commenced performing certain tasks. Recovering his shotgun from the floor, he reloaded both chambers. Next he replaced the empty cartridge in his revolver. In addition to his own shoulder rig, he also had Amos's Colt tucked in the front of his belt and so he checked this as well. To someone of a more imaginative turn of mind, he might easily have resembled one of the infamous pistol fighting irregulars of the Civil War.

The question was, what to do next?

His Winchester carbine languished in the leather scabbard on his horse, which was tethered in the trees to the side of the cabin. He had to assume that the riders were hostile. If they weren't, then life was being unusually kind to him. As the hoof beats drew nearer, Rance realized that he wouldn't have time to vacate the cabin, recover his horse and get away unnoticed. Therefore he had to bide his time and wait on events, which was always the hardest thing to do.

In a scene dreadfully reminiscent of the bunkhouse fight, he backed off to the far wall, taking the cabin's rudimentary table with him. Upending this, he crouched on the floor and pulled it in front of him. He held a vague hope that the newcomers would discover the dead body and assume that his killer had ridden off. If they then seized Rance's horse as a lucky windfall and departed well satisfied, it would be a heavy price to pay, but at least he would be left alone. Such far-fetched wonderings were a consequence of the tricks that played on a man's mind during

131

the hours of darkness, because the logical part of his brain simply told him that he had a fight on his hands.

The horsemen reined up in front of the cabin. 'Someone get a fire going in there,' boomed an authoritative voice. 'If I don't get me a cup of coffee soon, I'm going to butcher all the horses and go back to robbing banks!'

Following on from that, there was a flicker of light through the window as a Lucifer briefly flared into life. The speaker obviously considered himself above foraging for fuel and was apparently lighting a cigarette.

As Rance hunkered down behind the table, one of the men barged the door open and sauntered in. Two things then happened in quick succession. Out in the trees behind the cabin, a voice cried out, 'Hell's teeth, boss, there's a horse tethered back here!'

Then the lone intruder gave out a yelp of surprise as his boots encountered Tucker's body. 'Sweet Jesus, there's a stiff in here.'

The discoveries were greeted by a harsh tone of command. 'Drag the sucker out here so we can get a look at him. You fellows leave that goddamned animal alone and get the makings together. We need some light!'

Without looking closely at his surroundings, the nervous interloper grabbed hold of Tucker's boots and heaved him across the threshold. Almost immediately an aggrieved voice sounded shrilly. 'Hey, that's my partner, Amos!' There was a moment's reflection which was followed with, 'I'm puzzled by this, for Christ's sake. This just ain't right. He wasn't even here when that bitch lit out.'

Some measure of understanding and a great deal of anger suddenly flowed through Rance Toller, but he held himself in check. Crouched there in the darkness, his forehead greasy with sweat, it was obvious to him that the men were outlawed up, but there was a far more important consideration. He now knew of Billy Bob's whereabouts, but not Angie's and he couldn't cut loose with the sawn-off until he discounted her presence in the group. Luckily he didn't have long to wait.

Jake Ridgeway chuckled before responding. 'The way she was spurring that horse of hers, she's probably in Canada now. Unless Cole's bullet took the wind out of its sails, that is.' He looked over at him and sniggered, but Tucker was strangely pre-occupied.

'So if *she* didn't kill this sack of shit, who did?' Hastings pondered aloud. 'And just who does that horse belong to?'

Rance had heard enough. The men obviously intended staying the night, so his discovery was only a matter of time. His only chance was to strike first. And that chance came as the men got a fire going near the cabin entrance. As the flames took hold on the dry sticks, their night vision was abruptly ruined. Closing one eye, Rance got to his feet and moved swiftly over to the window.

A small group of men were clustered near the fire, whilst their leader remained on his horse, drawing on a smoke and peering suspiciously at his surroundings. Without any warning, their hidden assailant fired one barrel at the fire and the other directly at Cole Hastings. The powder flashes from the devastating blasts eerily lit up the night and then the screaming started. Someone had obviously taken a direct hit, but it certainly wasn't the outlaws' leader. He possessed the reactions of a scalded cat. Even as the first detonation rang out, Hastings was sliding out of his saddle. Of the second deadly load, most of the balls either struck his horse or flew off into the trees. Only one piece of lead actually hit him, but it did manage to tear a deep furrow across the front of his nose.

With his ears ringing, Rance swiftly replaced the spent cartridges. Knowing that he stood little chance of survival in the cabin, he then burst through the open door and raced towards his horse. Having retained some night vision, he avoided the total confusion around the small fire.

Even though in great pain from his damaged nose, Hastings knew instinctively what their adversary was about. Drawing a revolver, he bellowed out, 'Don't let him reach his horse, goddamn it!'

The man who had discovered the animal suddenly spotted the bulky figure running towards him and levelled his revolver. Since he was directly in line with Rance's horse, that individual couldn't risk using the shotgun. Instead, their lone foe abruptly dived off into the undergrowth just as the handgun fired. The bullet struck the ground behind where he had just been and then Rance, now at a favourable angle, emptied both barrels at the unfortunate outlaw. The combined blast quite literally reduced his torso to a bloody pulp and suddenly the way was clear for his killer to mount up.

With darkness as his shield, Rance charged towards his horse, but he hadn't reckoned on Cole Hastings' calculated ruthless streak. Without hesitation, the outlaw's leader conquered the intense pain in his face and took swift aim at the animal's dark bulk. Firing three times in rapid succession, he attained a remarkably close grouping. The bullets punched into soft flesh, so that the beast's screams merged with those of the shotgun's first victim.

As the stricken beast toppled over, Rance cursed bitterly and changed direction again. He was running out of options; even in the dark he couldn't hope to outrun mounted men. His only chance was to hit and run and try to wear down his adversaries. Disappearing into the deep shadows behind the cabin, he swiftly reloaded the scatter-gun as he listened to the initial reactions to his vicious assault. He had definitely accounted for two of the nightriders, although from the amount of screaming, one of them was a long time dying.

With blood coating his face, Cole Hastings was consumed by a form of cold rage that would tolerate no argument from anyone. His piercing eyes searched out Jake Ridgeway and red-tinged spittle flew from his lips as he barked out, 'Get back to the herd. I want another ten men over here pronto. Pick anyone that's good

137

with a gun. Tell the rest of them to move the horses south of here and then to wait for me. Savvy?'

Jake was dubious. 'Are you right sure about that, Cole? That son of a bitch could sit out there in the dark and carve us up one by one. You've set him afoot. Why not just leave him to the wolves?'

Hastings' response to that was to abruptly point his revolver at his own man. 'That whore's son has damn near torn my nose off. *No one* does that to me! And if you didn't have shit for brains, you'd know that wolves are afraid of humans. So just get the hell out of here and do what I told you!'

As his chastened employee rode off, Hastings switched his attention to his remaining men. 'Hit the dirt and stay there. I'm going to give us a bit of light to see by.' So saying, he bent double and rushed for the fire. Grabbing a burning branch, he then made for the empty cabin. Once inside, the outlaw was safe from attack and so took his time in making sure that the flames took hold. It was only when the front wall around the window was properly alight that he backed out and retreated into the shadows.

Mopping his wrecked nose with a kerchief, Hastings bellowed out into the darkness, 'I don't know who you are, mister, but you're going to rue the day you tangled with me. I'm a federal officer and pretty soon you're going to be surrounded by marshals. So do yourself a favour and give up now.'

Knowing that such barefaced lies were meant to draw out an unguarded response, Rance remained silent. He was still crouching behind the cabin, but knew that he couldn't remain there. The timber was beginning to crackle as flames moved up to the roof and the whole area would soon be bathed in light. Getting to his feet, he drew in a deep breath and sprinted for the trees. Desperate to cover some distance, he was suddenly very aware of the dead weight of his various weapons. Heavily armed men just weren't suited to any kind of running.

Perversely, it was actually bad light

that halted his progress. He had travelled maybe ten yards when his left foot got caught in a raised root and he sprawled helplessly forward. It was a chance encounter that most definitely saved his life. Just as he hit the ground, a rifle cracked behind him and he felt a blast of pressure as the bullet travelled close overhead.

'I nailed the bastard!' came a gleeful, but woefully mistaken cry. Hastings' jubilant marksman leapt up and bounded towards his victim, intent on being the first to rob the body.

'Get down, you moron,' yelled his boss, but it was too late. You didn't get any second chances with Rance Toller.

Rapidly twisting around, that man retracted both hammers of his shotgun and pointed it at the fast approaching runner. It just wasn't necessary to take deliberate aim with such a fearsome weapon. It was only as the gaping muzzles raised up in front of him that the trail-hand realized his terrible mistake and by then it was far too late.

With a distinctive roar, both barrels

belched forth bloody death and the hapless individual went down without a sound. Briefly obscured by a cloud of powder smoke, Rance took the opportunity to pile on the pressure. 'You fellows are all played out,' he yelled. 'Why don't you just move on while you still can?'

As the opposition digested that, he crawled back a few feet. A reply was not long in coming. 'That's a real crowd-pleaser you've got there,' remarked Hastings with a strangely brittle calm. 'How's about you bring it closer for me to look at?'

Despite killing three men, Rance still felt a burning resentment at the loss of his horse. Unless he managed to seize another, he would be in real trouble in such desolate country. With only two men left out there he was not going to get a better opportunity for some very brutal rustling. Because then there was Angie. For some reason, one of those fellows had taken a shot at her, which was reason enough for him to kill every last one of them.

And yet that damned inferno was gradually turning night into day. Another problem became apparent when he reloaded the sawn-off from the dwindling supply of cartridges in his pocket. Most of his spare ammunition was in the saddlebags that were strapped to his dead horse, so he really couldn't maintain a prolonged firefight.

He was just on the point of shifting position again when he heard the sound of drumming hoofs. With a sinking heart he realized that reinforcements were apparently arriving. He had obviously tangled with the vanguard of a big outfit and the odds were now definitely stacked against him. As the riders swept into the clearing beaten down in front of the blazing cabin, Hastings couldn't resist bellowing out a gratuitous offer. It helped to take his mind off the almost unbearable searing pain in his nose.

'I reckon my army's suddenly a whole lot bigger than yours, stranger, so I'll tell you something. If you shuck your shells and come over here real slow, you just might get to see another sunrise.' Lowering his voice, he then said to Jake Ridgeway, 'You take five men on a wide sweep round the back of that cockchafer and then move in on foot. That way, if he gets up, he'll be highlighted by the fire and you'll have him cold. The rest of you spread out near me.'

Hidden in the undergrowth, Rance watched as the new arrivals complied. He was unmoved by their boss's dubious offer and knew exactly what they were about. If he didn't make a move immediately he would be hopelessly trapped. With grim determination he looped the two-shoot gun over his head and right shoulder, drew both belt guns and retracted the hammers.

As the six horsemen moved into position behind him, Rance suddenly burst from cover and did the exact opposite of what anyone could have expected. Moving like a man possessed, he raced back towards the raging inferno, secure in the knowledge that no one on the other side of that was likely to spot him.

Those men to his rear were taken completely by surprise and could do little other than bellow out vague warnings. As he approached the doomed cabin, the heat became intolerable, but it wasn't his intention to loiter. Abruptly, Rance veered off to his right and suddenly found himself facing a dismounted and very surprised trail-hand.

As that man desperately tried to draw a bead on the lethal apparition, a shot rang out and a bullet struck him just left of centre. Cole Hastings glanced over in disbelief as his man spun round under the impact, but couldn't even make out where the shot had come from. 'Watch out,' he hollered furiously. 'The bastard's using the fire as cover.'

With his hair quite literally singeing, Rance pressed on again. As the fast-moving fugitive burst into view from the other side of the conflagration, he rapidly fired both revolvers. For those luckless new arrivals facing him, it was like encountering a vision straight from hell. Powder flashes erupted out of the night, interspersed with leaping tongues of flame. No one was actually hit, but the fusillade served to unnerve everyone. Rather than return fire, they all hit the dirt ... fast!

Scattered shots began to ring out from those men stationed on the far side of the cabin, but they were too far away for accurate fire. With the lead kicking up earth around him, Rance kept on firing as he made towards his dead horse. For Cole Hastings, who understood exactly what the lone gunman intended, it was all too much. As his revolver bucked repeatedly in his hand, he bellowed out in frustration, 'For Christ sake, he's just one man. Drop him before he uses that poxy animal as a fort!'

With his heart pounding fit to burst, Rance reached his objective and gratefully dropped down behind the protective bulk. Discarding his revolvers as though they were hot coals, he dragged his Winchester carbine out of its scabbard and suddenly Hastings' men were in serious trouble. Illuminated by the blazing cabin, they now faced a deadly foe firing a long gun from cover. And yet Rance didn't immediately open fire. He levered in a cartridge and then allowed his breathing to moderate before squeezing off a round.

With his first shot he knocked one of his assailants off his feet. As a steady stream of bullets came at them, Hastings' men soon found themselves impotently hugging the ground. Their belligerent leader was almost beside himself with frustration. All pretence of being a lawman was forgotten, yet he still had the sense to try to distract their deadly opponent. 'Goddamn it! Just who the hell are you, mister?' he bawled angrily. 'If you're carrying federal warrants, let's talk. You can't be after all of us and we could maybe do a deal.'

Ignoring the aggrieved looks from those nearest to him, Hastings gestured frantically for those men at the rear of the cabin to come around on Rance's flank. Oblivious to this and taking the opportunity to reload all his weapons from the ammunition in his saddle-bags, that man indulged in a little small talk. 'Why does everyone in this territory assume that I'm a lawman?'

'You mean you ain't?' responded a genuinely incredulous Hastings. 'So what the hell are we fighting for? I could use a man like you.'

'Then you shouldn't have taken a shot at my woman, you ass boil,' Rance retorted coldly. 'That made it personal, along with the killing of my horse.'

'Hey, he's the one that's working for that old bastard, Meeker, down in Browns Park,' hissed Billy Bob helpfully, before nausea and general weakness finally got the better of him. 'Don't that beat all?' he muttered dreamily, as the welcoming balm of unconsciousness crept over him. Blood loss and trauma meant that he was unlikely to ever wake up again.

Cole Hastings shook his head in disbelief. He had a herd to move and really didn't have time for all this shit. 'Ain't that the truth?' he responded wearily. Then a combination of pain and anger fired him up again. Hastily reloading his weapon, he barked at his men. 'Jake's coming in from the side. Throw everything you've got at that bastard!'

A volley of shots rang out and Rance had no option other than to cower down behind the inert bulk of his horse. He could feel the bullets thumping into its lifeless flesh and suddenly realized the reason for the burst of murderous activity. The group of men off to his right had to be moving in for the kill. The overwhelming numbers arrayed against him were finally beginning to tell. Such was the quantity of hot lead coming his way that he couldn't even risk a quick look. Despairingly, he did the only thing left to him. Taking up the scattergun, he eased it above his makeshift parapet and prepared for the worst. At least he would sell his life dearly!

9

It was Charlie Peach who first discovered that there was some form of mysterious conflict taking place. The buck-skin-clad scout didn't normally approve of travelling after dark; it was just too dangerous in so many ways. But Chad Seevers was a push-hard and in any case it appeared as though, on this occasion, there might just be something to be gained from it. The herd of stolen animals that they had been gradually overhauling was so vast that it was easy to track, whatever the conditions. He just had to be very careful that he didn't bump into one of the outriders in the Stygian gloom.

Charlie had gotten pretty damn close when suddenly, off to his right, all hell seemed to break loose. Muzzle flashes were clearly visible, as the sound of gunfire reverberated through the cool night air. Dismounting in some trees a short distance from the nearest of Hastings' trail-hands, he decided to wait on events and he wasn't disappointed. A lone rider appeared, barked out a few orders and then headed back they way he had come with close on a dozen men. It was as he watched them depart that Charlie noticed that the night sky to the west possessed a strange orange glow that had nothing to do with nature. It occurred to him that his boss now had his best chance yet of recovering the stolen horses.

Carefully making his way back to the main body of riders, Charlie sensibly announced his presence before rejoining them. Even in the murk, his perceptive employer could sense that he had news. 'Out with it, Charlie,' demanded the Bar S owner. 'Is it them?'

The scout nodded his head with obvious satisfaction. 'Oh yeah, it's them all right, Mister Seevers. And they've got involved in some kind of scrap over yonder, which means that the herd is plenty short of guards right now. Those murdering varmints must be after a juicy prize, but that ain't our problem, is it?'

The question seemed to hang in the air and he was mighty glad that the ultimate decision wasn't his to make.

Seevers glanced at his ramrod, Buck Slidell, and favoured him with a tight smile. 'So we've finally caught up with that ass boil,' he remarked tersely. 'We'll follow Charlie in until we're up close and then take back what's ours. If you have to fire, shoot to kill!'

As they moved off, he searched the darkness for Angie Sutter's diminutive figure and motioned for her to join him. As she willingly pulled alongside, the rancher favoured her with more than idle interest. Everything about her appealed to him. The story that she had related was remarkable enough and certainly ensured that they were on the same side. She was obviously a strong-willed and self-possessed young woman, who also conveniently happened to own a very trim figure and open, pretty features.

It had taken very little time for him to decide to supply her with a horse and all the food she could eat. He hoped that he would be able to continue doing that for a considerable spell, because very few women of such quality came anywhere near the Bar S ranch. Although genuinely sympathetic over the brutal slaying of her man, he couldn't help but think that providence must have dropped her in his lap. And he was going to make damn sure that no harm came to her.

'When we move in on those pus weasels, I want you to stay well back, you hear?'

Angie responded with a genuine smile, but there was a slight edge to her voice when she replied. 'I appreciate your concern, but I'm not a child, Mister Seevers. So don't you go treating me like one, you hear?'

His eyes narrowed slightly. If any of his hands had responded like that, he would have tipped them out of the saddle. Yet in her case it only seemed to add to her allure. 'OK, OK.' He held his hands up in mock surrender before continuing. 'But at least call me Chad. You're not on wages like the rest of them.'

Before she had chance to respond, Seevers suddenly cocked his head to one side and then spurred forward to close in on his scout. Shooting was plainly audible now and a rather foolish notion had crept into his head, because underneath his tough exterior there lay a genuinely decent personality. The thought of leaving some innocent folks to be slaughtered just didn't sit well with him.

As he joined Charlie Peach, that man waved him down. Speaking softly, the scout said, 'The herd's just over there, boss. We won't get a better chance.'

'Well I'm probably going to regret this,' Seevers offered gruffly, 'but those animals will have to keep for a while. I'm going over yonder to pick a fight. Tell the others to follow me and choose their targets carefully. We don't want to shoot the people we're trying to save!'

Peach recognized the set to his jaw and knew that there was only one suitable response. 'Oh shit!' he remarked dolefully, before doing exactly as instructed.

Rance Toller recognized that his time had come. After surviving twenty mostly hard years behind a badge, he was about to die in the middle of nowhere, fighting a bunch of low-life gun thugs for no discernible reason. Bullets continued to pepper his blood-soaked 'fort' and the predators on his flank were almost upon him. Forced to remain low, he couldn't even return fire.

With grim resolve, his fingers tightened on the twin triggers. As a head and shoulders loomed into view, he fired once and then again. Even over the roar of the second discharge, he could hear the horrendous screams of at least one victim. Desperately, he threw the heavy weapon up towards the remaining men and then reached for his revolvers. Tensing against the expected blizzard of lead, he waited … and waited.

Firing on his flank seemed to intensify, but it was all at a distance. Taking a chance, he snatched a quick look over his fleshy parapet. Even as he watched, one man was cut down and the rest fled towards their leader over beyond the still burning cabin. It suddenly dawned on Rance that, quite unbelievably, another force had entered the fray and that as a consequence everything had changed.

Cole Hastings stared uncomprehendingly at the muzzle flashes as they flared up from a completely unexpected quarter. For a brief crazy moment he thought it just might be some of his own men addled by drink, but then logic prevailed. As his three remaining flankers came running for cover, he realized that the situation was untenable. They were up against an unknown number of attackers, whilst his own dead and wounded littered the field of battle, leaving him severely disadvantaged. Cursing bitterly at the sudden reverse, Hastings did the only sensible thing and ordered a retreat. As those that could ran for any available horse, he peered resentfully over at the lone antagonist and filled his lungs.

'You hear me, mister? Whoever you are, when we meet again, *and we will*, I'm going to crush you flatter than hammered shit!'

Having uttered that improbably colourful threat, he mounted up and fled into the gloom along with his men. His sole priority was to get the herd moving out of harm's way, but as fresh spasms of pain tore through his nose, he knew that that night's work was most definitely unfinished. The only trouble was, he hadn't really got a good look at the man responsible and that fact might well come back to haunt him.

Chad Seevers reckoned that they'd come out of it pretty well, all things considered. Night actions were notoriously difficult to control and yet Hastings' gunslingers had been put to flight without the Bar S men taking a single casualty. Their efforts had not been in vain either, as at least one of those under attack was still alive. It wasn't long, though, before events started to take an extraordinary and disconcerting turn. As he and his men viewed the eerily shocking carnage by firelight, Seevers began to realize that only one man was responsible and that he now calmly awaited them beyond the cabin.

The man standing behind the blood-drenched animal was a well-built individual of around six feet. He was reloading a wicked-looking sawn-off and it was only when he had completed his task that he deigned to return their scrutiny. As the rancher looked into his eyes, Seevers was struck by the aura of latent violence that seemed to surround the lone gunman, but he did prove to possess a civil tongue.

'I'm much obliged to you fellows. Reckon they had me by the throat there, towards the end.' And then, as though by way of explanation to a new set of strangers, he added somewhat lamely, 'I guess they just took against me.'

Before anyone could respond to that nonsense, there was a strangled cry from the rear and then Angie's figure burst through the cordon of riders. For a moment, she stared owlishly at the solitary figure before exclaiming, 'Sweet Jesus, I thought you was dead for sure!'

Then, as Seevers and his men looked on in amazement, she flung herself bodily at Rance. Momentarily lost for words, that man wrapped his arms around her and hugged long and hard. There was a desperation in her grip that spoke volumes and he suddenly realized that she had given him up for dead. Finally, he came up for air and eased back slightly, enough to offer his own particular brand of greeting. Gazing warmly down at her, he remarked, 'You took your sweet time about it, lady!'

And then the two of them burst out laughing, which in its way was as much about releasing tension as sharing humour. It was only when Chad Seevers noisily cleared his throat that either of them recognized that they really should offer some sort of explanation. Placing an arm affectionately around her man, Angie favoured the rancher with a rejuvenated smile.

'Chad, this is Rance Toller, the man

that I told you about. The man that I was convinced had been killed in that bunkhouse fire.'

The rancher sat his horse and stared down at her in disbelief. Behind his dead-pan expression was a mind in seething turmoil.

'Looks like you nearly got fried again, mister,' remarked Buck Slidell wryly. He felt beholden to say something, seeing as his boss, having got their attention, was now so uncharacteristically silent.

'I seem to be attracted to fires,' Rance responded lightly. His remark had been addressed to the ramrod, but his eyes never left Seevers' face. That man, who was obviously the leader, remained strangely mute, so that even Angie's ebullience was beginning to fade. Then a shout from close by attracted everyone's attention.

'We've got a live one here, boss. Looks like he's taken quite a battering. What would you have us do?'

Rance's response was unequivocal. 'He doesn't deserve considerations. Let him bleed out!'

Everybody's attention, with the exception of Rance and Angie, who had returned to gazing at each other, turned to Chad Seevers. They weren't used to seeing their leader second-guessed and that man finally found his voice. 'I reckon that's only fitting. Him being a shootist and horse thief both.' Glancing over at his scout, he added, 'Charlie, get yourself out there and make sure that Hastings has backed right off.' Only then did he return his full attention to Angie's new companion. 'We've been trailing these buzzards from near Douglas, Wyoming. We'd have had them tonight, only we saved your skin instead, so I'd kind of like to hear your story. If you're up to it, that is.'

Rance favoured him with a cool smile. 'Something's eating at this guy,' he muttered to himself, before replying, 'since you put it like that, I guess you've got every right.'

With Angie still clinging tightly to him, he moved closer to the fire and waited for the rancher to join them. Then, in a professional and almost detached manner, he related all that had happened to him since the fight in the bunkhouse. Seevers heard him out in silence, although his eyes widened at the news of Ray Spence's demise; even up in Wyoming, they'd heard of him. As Rance fell silent, the rancher nodded with grudging admiration.

'You certainly carry a big stick, Mister Toller. The question is, what are your intentions now?' As he spoke, an empty pit opened up in his stomach. Whatever the answer to that, he recognized that his chances of any kind of future relationship with Angie had dropped to a big, fat zero.

'My friends call me Rance,' that man responded. 'And since I'm on foot, I'm kind of in your hands. However, my preference is to tag along with you. Those bastards killed my horse and fired on Angie and their *amigos* down in Browns Park kidnapped her, so I reckon there's things need setting right. *And* you might could just use an extra gun when you catch up with your horses.'

For the first time that night, Seevers allowed a faint smile to cross his face. 'I'll allow that we could certainly benefit from a man of your ... talents, *Mister Toller.* We brought along some spare mounts. I'll tell Buck to get you fixed up.' With that, he nodded and strode away, back straight and shoulders square as usual. He figured that the two of them would want some time alone and in truth he really didn't want to be around Angie for a while. The onset of bitter disappointment was actually making his heart ache.

Buck Slidell was oblivious to his boss's mental anguish and so didn't realize that he would have been best holding his tongue. 'I reckon you called it just right, boss, stepping in on this bloodbath rather than going for the herd. Those thieving cockchafers got plenty thinned out tonight. That'll count when we finally bring them to heel.'

Seevers rounded on his subordinate with far greater ferocity than he had ever intended. 'And what if we don't catch them until they reach Browns Park?

They'll join forces with Bassett's men and then we'll really be up against it. And all because we saved some lethal drifter. Did you think about that, *hey*?'

He almost shouted the last sentence and some of his men peered over curiously. As for Rance and Angie, well they were wrapped up in their own world, but Rance was never completely oblivious to his surroundings. The ex-lawman caught the rancher's mood and did just wonder whether outlaws were the only folks that he would have to contend with back in Browns Park.

10

It was late the following afternoon when Nelson Cross finally arrived at Bassett's ranch. Not wishing to over tire his horse, he had deliberately taken his time, which of course was all the easier without having a companion to chivvy him along. The lush grass in the valley was a welcome change from the barren terrain around Robbers' Roost and he decided that he just might hang around for a while, whatever the outcome of his summons.

'You took your damn time,' grumbled Herb Bassett by way of a greeting. 'And what the hell happened to Klee? I didn't tell him he could go off on a celebray.'

'Who?' asked Cross, cocking his head slightly to one side, which only served to emphasize the dreadful scar tissue on his neck.

'The messenger I sent out to come and get you,' Bassett responded impatiently.

164

'Oh, him,' the shootist answered innocently. 'Well I'll tell you something. You ought to put him out to grass. The old buzzard was tuckered out. Slept like a baby. Thought it best to let him lie, seeing as he worked for you, and all.'

Herb Bassett rubbed a meaty paw over his features, as was his habit when under pressure. He was faced with an obvious lie, but had more on his mind than just the welfare of an ageing employee. And he had to take into account the calibre of the man before him; it wasn't wise to voice doubt in the word of a man like Nelson Cross.

'Well anyhoo, I reckon you'll want to wash up and set a spell. Eat, drink your fill and get a good night's sleep. Come morning, I need you to ride over to Wes Meeker's spread. Young Johnny will show you the way.'

'What's this Meeker to you?' inquired Cross with a vague stirring of interest. If his services were required so soon, then it likely meant the spilling of blood.

'I'll tell you all about it inside, but

think on this. It was in front of Meeker's ranch house that Ray Spence drew his last breath. I've been shorthanded around here since then, but of course now that you're here...'

'I think you'd better see this, boss.'

Wes Meeker looked up sharply. It was early morning and the two men had just had their first coffee of the day. There was a nervous edge to Jackson's voice that was reminiscent of the night of the bunkhouse fight. Grabbing a Winchester, the rancher moved rapidly over to the door and peered out. The sun had edged up over the horizon only a short while before, but the light was amply sufficient.

The lone rider was still some way off, but close enough for the two men to see that he was clad in black from head to toe: hat, frock coat, trousers, boots and gloves. Hell, even his ample stubble appeared to be black. There was a steady, menacing quality to his approach that reminded both of them of when Ray Spence had come calling.

'I wish Rance was here,' Meeker muttered softly and then instantly regretted it. He hated displaying any form of weakness, but he knew that he just hadn't got the stomach for vicious, close-up gunplay. It seemed that the older he got, the more he wanted to live.

As Nelson Cross drew level with the charred remains of the bunkhouse, a fleeting smile graced his brutalized features. 'Looks like you've been having some ill luck, boys,' he called out with fake geniality. 'What was it, a lightning strike?'

Meeker managed to sound a lot tougher than he felt. 'You know damn well what caused it, you ghoul,' he barked out. 'Get the hell off my property while you still can!'

Cross merely shook his head and kept on coming. 'You can't kill the messenger,' he calmly remarked, ''cause that way you'll never get the message.'

Raw fear was eating at Meeker, but he tried to mask it with bravado. 'Well then have your say and go, but first I want to know what happened to Angie,' he retorted, ostentatiously levering up a cartridge. By his side he heard Jackson do the same. Surely this unnerving son of a bitch wouldn't chance his hand against two cocked rifles. With the awning along the front of the house, the men were stood in shade, thereby giving them a welcome edge.

'Don't know no Angie and believe me, if I *had* met her we'd both remember,' Cross remarked with a smirk as he slowly dismounted. 'Anyhoo, back to business. Mister Bassett wants you to see reason. He can't understand why a man like you would choose to live on the Outlaw Trail, it being so full of *bad* people an' all.' Keeping his right hand well away from the Colt Navy at his waist, he carefully eased off the leather glove. 'He told me not to kill you unless you flat out refused to co-operate, but you know what?'

Despite the sickening tension, the rancher couldn't hide his curiosity. Coated with sweat, Meeker stared at the man before him, all the while hoping desperately to defuse the situation.

'My name's Nelson Cross and I rarely do as I'm told,' that man spat out. At the same time, his right hand moved so fast that it was just a blur. The cap n' ball revolver cleared leather and was triggered so rapidly that Wesley Meeker didn't even have time to react. An out-dated, but still deadly lead ball punched unerringly into the bone and gristle that had once been his nose and kept on going. His life was snuffed out in a welter of blood and brain matter. The variable light had made not a jot of difference to the cold-eyed professional.

Spattered by his former employer's lifeblood, Jackson dropped his rifle to the ground as though it was a hot coal and threw himself on the assassin's mercy. 'For pity's sake don't shoot me, mister. I didn't do anything!'

'Well you should have,' Cross retorted in a fair attempt at black humour. His Colt crashed out again and the ranch-hand gazed in horror at the blood suddenly spewing from the agonizing hole in his stomach. As reaction set in, he fell back against the heavy open door and then slid uncontrollably to the floor.

Cross smirked as he sauntered across the threshold. 'I'm told belly wounds really concentrate the mind. You'll have to let me know what you think,' he added conversationally. With that, he moved carefully on into the house looking for any other occupants. The sound of pounding hoofs reached his ears, confirming that at least one more individual had decided not to trade lead with him. Reaching the rear of the substantial building, he peered out through a window and saw another ranch-hand scurrying for the stables. 'They're like rats fleeing a sinking ship,' he thought.

It was a long shot for any revolver and the distance was widening with every second, but the gunfighter didn't hesitate. He took pleasure in killing and had no scruples whatsoever about shooting a man in the back. Aiming straight between the shoulder blades, he gently squeezed the curved trigger. With a satisfying crash, a third chamber detonated, sending Meeker's sole remaining employee tumbling to the ground.

'I enjoyed that,' Cross announced to the empty room.

As the stricken man coughed up gobbets of blood, his killer looked around for a kerosene lamp. The sight of the blackened bunkhouse had provided him an amusing idea. 'Why not finish the job?'

Jackson stared through watery eyes as his executioner re-appeared. A sea of pain deluged his broken body, but even so he couldn't believe what he was witnessing. The black-clad fiend was using a Lucifer to light the wick of an oil lamp.

'You might want to shuffle off to Hades or wherever it is that you're going,' that man helpfully suggested, 'because it's going to be as hot as hell around here soon!'

With that, he turned up the flame and nonchalantly heaved the lamp at the table. The highly flammable liquid ignited immediately and fire soon took hold on the dry, seasoned timber.

'For God's sake, you can't leave me like this,' pleaded the mortally wounded man. 'At least give me a gun, to end it!'

'Yeah, but where would be the fun in that?' asked the gunman. A sick look had entered his eyes as he regarded his victim with far more than just professional interest. 'I really would like to stay around and have a chin wag, but it's getting mighty hot in here.' So saying, Cross cautiously stepped outside and scrutinized his surroundings. The ranch had obviously been short-handed, because there didn't appear to be anyone left, which in a way was rather disappointing.

With flames spreading rapidly, it wasn't long before high-pitched screams emanated from the house. Cross laughed out loud and returned to where his horse was patiently waiting. It occurred to him that, for all his fearsome reputation, Ray Spence couldn't really have been up to much to be stopped by such feeble opposition.

His ever-watchful eyes spotted Bassett's hand stationed on the ridge. He realized that the beefy outlaw leader would likely be riled up when he heard of his murderous tactics and decided there and then to pass some time by indulging in a little private enterprise. There was some fine-looking horseflesh in Meeker's corral that no longer had an owner. Cross, who of course had found out about the massive herd on its way south, knew that Cole Hastings would be happy to sell them to the US Cavalry on his behalf. They were old *compadres* who shared a wary appreciation of each other's lethal talents.

Nodding with satisfaction, he made for the corral. By the time he returned, Bassett would have calmed down and he would collect for a job well done. After all, the big man finally possessed the free grazing that he needed!

Herb Bassett stared at his scout in stunned disbelief.

'I saw it with my own eyes, boss,' the man insisted. 'Apart from one hand that got away, Cross killed everything on two legs and then torched the place.'

'And now where is he?' demanded the outlaw leader heatedly.

'He cleaned out the corral. Last I saw of him, he was headed north.'

'The son of a bitch is a maniac, but I'll allow he's got half a brain,' muttered Bassett. 'He knows that if those animals are mixed in with Hastings' herd, then it's a done deal and I won't be able to lay claim to them.'

He suddenly glanced around at the minions surrounding him and realized that he was talking too much. It didn't pay to divulge his thoughts in front of lesser mortals. The pressure involved in such a big money scheme was obviously getting to him. If only he had had a strong son to accept some of the load.

After pacing up and down in silence for a while, the bear-like figure finally marshalled his thoughts. Turning to one of his men, he instructed, 'Jeb, take some men over to Meeker's. Any stiffs that survived the fire, I want them buried deeper than a coal seam. No traces. Nothing for any kind of law to find. You hear?'

'Yes, boss,' responded that man swiftly.

'Then take a scout around. See if there's any sign of the one that got away. I'll look mighty favourably on anyone who puts a bullet in him. Savvy?'

Before Jeb could even acknowledge that order, the solid main door swung open with a thump. Every man in the room stared at the newcomer in stunned surprise. The travel-stained and clearly ill-used figure of Klee stumbled into the room. He had a bloodied bandanna tied around his forehead and was obviously all but dead on his feet.

'That goddamned gunsel buffaloed me,' he announced shakily. 'Even emptied my pockets before he left. Tell me, where's the justice in that, Mister Bassett?' With that, his legs buckled beneath him and the aggrieved messenger collapsed on the floor.

Herb Bassett shook his head in baffled amazement. God help anyone who Nelson Cross took an active dislike to!

Cleatus Tubbs couldn't remember a

time when he'd been so scared. His sole instinct was to put as much distance between himself and that black-clad fiend as possible. With the frightening benefit of hindsight, he couldn't understand why he had stuck with old man Meeker for so long. The writing had been on the wall since Ray Spence had got himself obliterated by a twelve-gauge shotgun. And now Cleatus was quite literally running for his life!

For some reason the terrified ranch-hand had struck out to the north. He sensibly reckoned that, as the sole survivor and witness of a triple slaying, men would be coming after him to ensure his permanent silence. The more that thought worked on his fevered imagination, the more he realized that he might well have to travel an awful long way. Down south were the fearsome Apaches and beyond them the dubious delights of Mexico, whereas ahead of him lay, eventually, Canada. Cleatus hadn't heard anything bad about Canada, probably because it was a known fact that hardly anyone lived there. It never occurred to him that that might be because it was just so damned cold for most of the year.

For some time he kept his horse at a gallop, but eventually it dawned on his feverish mind that such a pace would kill the beast and set him afoot. Reluctantly, the nervous ranch-hand slowed right down to a walk and began to take more notice of his surroundings. It was this that almost certainly saved his life.

From the amount of noise and dust in the distance, there had to be a hell of a lot of something coming towards him. Then he spotted the single rider on point and it suddenly came to him. It just had to be the huge herd of stolen horses that Mister Meeker had mentioned. Cleatus realized that any encounter with that gang of rustlers would surely bring trouble and so he wisely veered off to his left and gave them a wide berth. It occurred to him that if he then came around behind them, such action would place the vast horde between him and any pursuers. Of course that would unknowingly place him directly in the path of the next band of horsemen!

Cole Hastings felt himself to be between 'a rock and a hard place' and he didn't like it one little bit. He knew damn well that the ass boils that had jumped him and his men two nights earlier were on his back trail. His raw instincts told him to take every man and hit back hard, but a voice in his head instructed him to bide his time. Left untended, the herd would quickly disintegrate and scatter across the territory. All the work and killing that it had taken to amass so many horses would go to waste. And yet the knowledge that they were being closely followed was unnerving his men, because it was generally them that did the intimidating.

'I don't like this one little bit,' snarled Jake Ridgeway with an almost uncanny appreciation of his boss's negative thoughts. Since their bloody reverse at the cabin, he had been noticeably less subservient. 'Why are those sons of bitches holding back? And why are we holding back? Time was you'd have been all over them like a bitch on heat!' He viewed his boss speculatively, as though he half suspected the answer. 'You ain't running scared are you, Cole?'

That man jerked slightly as a nerve twitched in his neck. 'Say what?' he rasped dangerously.

His butt-ugly companion failed to notice the signals and so continued to run off at the mouth. 'Only as I recall, your last killing was that young snotnose near Douglas and even my old ma could have done that one!'

Hastings shook his head regretfully as he motioned his horse over to the other man. His hands were apparently well clear of any weapon and even though his bloodied nose throbbed relentlessly, his features were curiously deadpan. Jake misread the approach as being one of conciliation and so maintained his belligerent expression. It was only as the other man drew level that doubt entered his thoughts and by then it was far too late.

Hastings threw himself sideways out

of the saddle, so that all his upper body weight slammed into his unprepared opponent. The momentum was sufficient to carry both men clean off their horses. They hit the unyielding ground with a sickening thump, but as intended it was Jake that bore the brunt of it. With the air crushed out of his lungs and a dead weight on his chest, he was quite suddenly as helpless as a baby. Hastings' right hand streaked towards his corresponding boot and came away with a wicked looking skinning knife. As the razor sharp point probed his victim's neck, his left hand seized a knot of lank, greasy hair.

'Don't ever back talk me again, you pathetic maggot,' snarled the outlaw leader. 'Or so help me, I'll open you up from ear to ear and then leave you to the buzzards, you hear?'

His prey was starved of oxygen and completely immobile. The only sound that came from his lips was a meaningless croak and yet Hastings was completely unmoved by his subordinate's suffering. Relentlessly bearing down, he added,

'Right now, this herd is all that counts. And if they're ever going to pass muster for the goddamned army paymaster, those animals need water and grazing. Once we reach Browns Park and the Green River, we can leave them with Bassett's men and take care of whoever's following us. But you won't be alive to see it if you don't back off!'

With his body starved of air, Jake's unshaven features were turning purple and his agonizing death was a real possibility. Even through his great distress, he could see that his boss was chillingly indifferent to his fate. What saved him was a completely unexpected intervention.

'If you get to fighting amongst yourselves, there's no hope for any of you,' remarked Nelson Cross sagely.

Cole Hastings jerked with surprise and twisted around to view the totally unforeseen new arrival. In so doing he unintentionally relieved some of the pressure on Jake's chest and thereby granted him life. As that man desperately sucked air into his lungs, his saviour moved in closer. Those trail-hands nearby had been totally mesmerized by Jake's suffering, which had allowed Cross to move in unobserved. He knew that Hastings would loath having been taken unawares and so allowed his right hand to hover conspicuously near his Colt. With instinctive perception, he had already removed the leather glove that protected his deadly extremity.

The two ruthlessly professional gunfighters eyed each other warily. Neither of them really knew which was the faster and in truth were not at all keen to find out. Most shootists avoided others of their own ilk and took on men of lesser ability, or else favoured ambush or even back-shooting.

After long moments of strained scrutiny, Hastings finally broke the silence. 'So what just happens to bring you here? And don't tell me it's a coincidence, because I don't believe in them.' With that, he carefully got to his feet and Jake's near-death experience was finally over.

Cross offered a mirthless smile as he

responded. 'There's a ranch over yonder needing a new owner. Out of concern for their welfare, I liberated some prime horseflesh that I thought you might sell for me. On commission, of course. And who knows, with all that's going on, you could need an extra gun around here as well.'

'Just who was the rancher?' Hastings queried casually, effectively hiding his sudden concern that it could be Herb Bassett. 'I might know him.'

'Old cuss, name of Meeker,' the black-clad gunman replied. 'He got kind of careless with some kerosene.' At that point he suddenly offered a dazzlingly authentic smile, which told Hastings all that he really needed to know.

That man felt a genuine surge of relief. Wesley Meeker meant little to him and his sudden death certainly did not affect his plans. In fact with him out of the way, there would be nothing to hinder the herd's arrival in Browns Park. All of which meant that he would not have to test his murderous reactions against those of Nelson Cross anytime soon. The uneasy peace between them could be maintained while everyone attended to business!

11

Rance Toller watched with growing impatience as the three men, Seevers, Buck and Charlie, held their council of war. He had been excluded by the simple act of not being invited, so he could only kick his heels with Angie on the sidelines. Not that spending time with her was any kind of chore, but there were things brewing and he was better qualified than most to get involved. Chad Seevers was undoubtedly a tough and capable man, but sometimes that simply wasn't enough. The former lawman was just about to butt in anyway, when one of Seevers' men rode into the temporary camp with a vaguely familiar companion.

'I kind of stumbled over this fella, boss. He's got one hell of a story to tell and that's no error.'

As everyone gathered around to listen, the nervous newcomer told of Wesley

Meeker's brutal demise and the subsequent destruction of the ranch house. Even though he hadn't actually witnessed it, he graphically described how the black-clad maniac had slaughtered the other two men.

Rance could recognize flowery language when he heard it, but it was obvious that the fugitive was essentially telling the truth and his blood began to boil. Shouldering his way through the idle ranch-hands, he strode directly up to the owner of the Bar S. Gesturing towards Cleatus Tubbs, he angrily stated, 'Well that just tears it! If what this fella says is true, then a good man got butchered this morning. According to Angie, his brother's widow and two children were going to come and live with him and now that's never going to happen.'

Seevers regarded Rance with ill-concealed impatience. 'Ill tidings to be sure, but I don't see how this alters anything. We were just working on a plan to tackle the bull turds that stole my horses.'

Rance struggled to control his own

irritation. 'With Meeker gone, there's nothing to stop those "bull turds" from taking over his spread, alongside the men that are behind the killings. Don't you see? They're all in it together. It's all about moving and selling a vast number of stolen stock. Your herd is just a small part of it.'

'So what would *you* have us do?' responded the rancher pointedly.

Rance took a deep breath and concentrated his thoughts. When he spoke again, he was calm and controlled, as though he had suddenly resumed his position as an experienced lawman. 'Your men answer to you, Mister Seevers. They respect you and they'll do what you tell them, but you see the thing is this: you're a rancher, not a shootist. If you go charging in after those men, you and your men will get to dying!'

'Just what are you saying?' rasped Seevers angrily.

'I'm saying that you're not outlawed up. Your business is animals. Oh yeah, some of your men might be good with a gun against snakes and such, but they're still just ranch-hands.' Gesturing towards the south, Rance added, 'Those fellas out there spend their time taking things from people. They kill folks when they need to and some of them even enjoy it. Believe me, I know.'

It was at that point that Angie moved up to join her man. As she spoke, she peered up earnestly at the owner of the Bar S. 'Listen to him, Chad. He does know what he's talking about. I was with him in Devils Lake last year and it was a sight to see.'

Seevers' eyes opened wide as he digested that. He still hadn't quite come to terms with the loss of a woman that he had set his heart on, but the news that they had been involved with that shindig made him realize just how unattainable she really was. 'That was you?' he inquired incredulously. Even in the remotest parts of the West, people had heard stories about the momentous gun battle in northern Dakota. Such an event must have created quite a bond between them.

Angie allowed Rance to take the lead again and he nodded silently. His expression was grave and it was some time before he offered a diffidently brief response. 'I ain't proud of it.'

Seevers stared intently at the two of them. It had suddenly dawned on him that the rather odd couple standing before him were actually very special indeed. In a rather lethal fashion. 'Seems like you're someone I really ought to take advice from,' he grudgingly allowed. 'So OK, what would you have us do, Rance?'

The other man recognized that such an admission hadn't come easily and so refrained from any display of satisfaction. Instead he got straight down to business.

'You need to accept that you're not just after a few horses. You've got at least one dead man back in Wyoming and Angie and I have got our own grievances, which means that we're all out for revenge. So there's going to be killing. Quite likely a lot of it.'

Rance was conscious that he now had everyone else's rapt attention. The buckskin-clad scout, the ramrod and all the ranch-hands were watching him intently as he continued. 'We'll let the herd reach Browns Park. I reckon they'll intend staying there for some time. Fatten the animals up and get them saddle-broke. They'll need Bassett and all his men for that, so we'll know exactly where everyone is. And we'll take advantage of that. It will give us chance to even the odds a bit.'

He paused briefly before settling his unblinking gaze on Chad Seevers. 'Anyone that doesn't want blood on their hands had better leave now, because I ain't carrying passengers.'

Those last words carried a chill that touched every man present and yet not one of them backed away ... except for Cleatus Tubbs, who began to shuffle about uncomfortably. Rance nodded with evident approval, before abruptly shifting his gaze on to the sole remaining Meeker employee. 'I reckon you happened on us by accident, hightailing it away from your boss's cremation. You were in no all-fired hurry to fight before, so I won't be pressing you now. *But,* you know the lie of the land down there and we don't, so I'll need you to act as a guide. You owe Wes that much at least. And when it's all over, you can carry on heading north, all the way to ... *Canada,* maybe.'

Cleatus coloured like a beetroot, but had the good sense to accept the situation without arguing. In fact, as attention moved away from him, his main reaction became puzzlement, 'How the hell did that son of a bitch know I was heading for the border?'

★   ★   ★

Herb Bassett sat his mount atop the ridge and watched in awe as the vast herd swept into the lush valley like a wave on a beach. The animals had smelt the water of the Green River and for the last few miles there had been no holding them back.

'Sweet Jesus, will you look at all that cash money?' he muttered to himself. He had to admit that Cole Hastings had buttered his bread on both sides this time.

The temporarily redundant outriders had given up trying to control the crazed animals and were following on behind through the dust. They all slouched wearily in their saddles, for all the world resembling hard-bitten, professional trail-hands, rather than the outlaws on the dodge that they actually were.

To Bassett's practised eye it appeared as though their numbers were a little on the low side for controlling such a large number of animals. Could they have run into trouble on their way south? Then his keen gaze took in the figures of Nelson Cross and Cole Hastings and his expression hardened. Taken as a pair, those two would be quite a handful, but it was the black-clad gunfighter who held his attention the most. That son of a bitch had gratuitously overstepped his instructions and then skipped off on his own account. Such behaviour was graphically emphasized by the still-smoking ruin of the ranch house below, which only served to irk him all the more. They could have used it as a base while saddle-breaking the horses and Wesley Meeker's slaughter might well carry repercussions. Kin could be funny about such things, if indeed he had any. And then there was that stranger, Rance. Whoever the hell he was. And where in blazes could he have got to?

Turning to the young gopher at his side, he commanded, 'Johnny, get yourself back to my spread and tell the men to get on over here, pronto. There's a lot of work to do and those fellows down there won't be up for it for a while. Just tell Lee and Chester to stick around to mind the store.'

As the young man raced off to do his bidding, Bassett reluctantly urged his mount down the steep slope towards the long awaited arrivals. He didn't relish doing business with the two independent-minded gun thugs, but needs must. It was as he neared the valley floor that he noticed his man Jeb and a couple of companions following the herd in. They looked uncomfortable when they spotted him and he guessed that the sole survivor of Cross's murder raid had eluded them.

'I'm real sorry, boss,' Jeb muttered regretfully. 'I never could track worth a damn and he must have tucked in behind all these horses.'

Bassett favoured him with a sour look. 'Well don't get comfy. All these horses are going to keep you and the boys busy for days to come.'

It was early evening when Charlie Peach and Cleatus Tubbs returned to the main party. They had been reconnoitring the valley, utilizing Cleatus's local knowledge.

'They've taken over Meeker's spread, what's left of it. They look pretty tuckered out to me,' reported the scout. 'But get this. Around twenty riders came in from the west just before we left. Cleatus reckons they must have emptied Bassett's ranch to do that.'

'Anything else?' demanded Seevers.

'Yeah,' remarked Charlie casually. 'There sure is some real pretty country hereabouts. As good as anything we've got in Wyoming.'

With the weight of command on his

shoulders, the rancher could only stare at him incredulously. 'Thanks,' he finally responded. 'I'll bear that in mind.' It was then that, almost as an afterthought, he turned to face Rance. 'So what do you reckon?'

That was exactly what that man had been waiting for. 'You're asking me?'

Seevers produced a great sigh as he bowed to the inevitable. He was a proud man, but he was no fool. 'Yes, I am.'

'Well thank you,' replied Rance, flashing a genuine smile, before allowing his mood to darken. 'Right then, you men. Listen up! If Bassett's got his cronies doing some bronc-busting, we're going to go where he ain't. We're outnumbered powerful bad, so we'll concentrate our numbers where they are weakest.'

'And do what?' demanded Seevers.

'Fight fire with fire. Bassett burnt Meeker out, so we'll return the favour.'

As the men gawped at him, Buck Slidell glanced briefly at his boss before posing a question. 'These men have been pushed real hard for days now. They're awful tired. Why not hunker down for the night and wait until tomorrow?'

A strange chill seemed to descend on Rance Toller. Every man present sensed the aura of menace that abruptly came over him. He eased slowly forward until he was almost touching the Bar S ramrod. His eyes were like flints as he softly responded. 'Those goddamned rustlers have been thieving and killing across any number of territories before driving the herd down here. Right now they'll be dead on their feet. So we're going to hit them hard and keep on hitting them until we've ripped the heart out of them.' His voice suddenly erupted as a great snarl. 'Savvy?'

Buck involuntarily took a step back and nodded quickly. He'd never encountered so much concentrated venom before and yet this guy was on the same side, for Christ's sake! Just who the hell was he, anyway?

As Rance turned away, he suddenly found himself confronted by Angie's delightful features. 'Don't be too hard on them. They're ranchers, not hired killers.'

His response was gentle, but unyielding. 'Well if they want to survive this, they're going to have to get mean — real mean!'

Cole Hastings viewed the charred remnants of the two buildings with distaste. 'This place don't look so good. All we wanted was grazing rights. Wouldn't it have been easier to just buy him off?'

Nelson Cross snorted with amusement and strolled away, leaving Herb Bassett to answer that one. The big man frowned with annoyance. He needed to have words with the black-clad gunfighter, but the time wasn't right. 'Meeker was a stubborn old fool and my hired help didn't take instruction ... as one of them found out to his cost.'

To Bassett's surprise, the horse thief displayed no distain for other people's failings. Instead he was deadly serious. 'Ray Spence took on the wrong man and so did we. Whatever he is, I aim to settle matters with him and those that helped him, but not right now. They're out there somewhere on our back trail, but tonight I just want to eat and sleep.' From under his sweat-stained slouch hat he fixed his hard eyes on Bassett. 'So there had better be some food laid on in this dump.'

The other man matched his stare, which was no easy task under the circumstances. The rustler's nose was really quite a picture, but Bassett chose not to inquire about just what had happened on the trail drive. That could wait for a while. Instead he replied forcefully, 'There's no call to get tetchy with me, Cole. I've had the men butcher some steers. There'll be all the steaks and beans you can eat over in the barn and there's plenty of room in there to bed down after.'

Hastings nodded grudgingly. 'Fair enough, Herb. Fair enough.' His next words were prophetic. 'I think you'll find that I'm in a far better humour by the morning.'

12

The grimly resolute band moved cautiously across the darkened landscape. Ahead of them lay an imposing ranch house with an unknown number of occupants. Arrayed around it were a bunkhouse, large barn and corral. They all knew that they had to keep well clear of the latter, so as not to spook the animals. It had already been decided that Rance and Chad Seevers would tackle the house, whilst the other men would be arrayed around the perimeter between the ranch and the bulk of the opposition on the Green River. Charlie Peach, because of his experience fighting Apaches, had been placed in charge of this group, which, minus two horse holders and an unsurprisingly absent Cleatus Tubbs came to nine men.

As Rance gave the signal to halt, he turned to Angie and whispered, 'You stay with the horse holders and *keep down*.'

She reacted with unexpected fire. Clutching a Winchester recovered from one of Hastings' slain riders, the young woman prodded him sharply in the chest with it.

'Like hell I will!' she retorted fiercely. 'I nearly lost you once. I ain't doing it again. Where you go, I go!'

As he peered at her through the gloom, he could sense the determined set to her features and reluctantly accepted the futility of arguing. In fact he was secretly proud of the gutsy young woman and that she should actually choose to be associated with him. And then it came to him. If she *had* to be part of the assault, then he might as well use her undoubted charms to facilitate it. 'Very well, but you do exactly as I say. Understand?'

She nodded silently.

'Say it!' he hissed belligerently.

'I understand,' she replied softly and then briefly clasped his hand. Despite the situation he warmly returned the pressure, but then the moment all too swiftly passed and it was back to business. If Angie had not been so pre-occupied, she might well have noticed the unusually intense gaze that Chad Seevers lavished on her. It had certainly crossed his jaundiced mind that this woman was far too valuable to be involved in such risky proceedings, but sadly he seemed to have no say in the matter.

Leaving the larger party in Charlie Peach's capable hands, the three of them moved soundlessly over to the substantial house. In reality it was simply a very big log cabin, built out of rough-cut timber in the traditional manner and divided into several rooms, but it was better by far than anything else in that part of the world. The yellowish glow from several oil lamps was visible through the windows. From inside, there came the sound of raucous laughter and Rance guessed that whoever remained in the building was making the best of Bassett's absence.

As they reached the main entrance, Rance murmured to Angie, 'Tell them you've got a message from Herb Bassett.'

She caught on immediately and he could make out her white teeth as the young woman smiled her assent. She waited until the two men had positioned themselves on either side of the door and then beat on it with the butt of her Winchester. For a moment there was total silence inside, but then heavy footfalls announced the arrival of at least one man at the other side of the heavy barrier.

'Who is it and what do you want?' demanded a gruff voice.

'I've got a message from Mister Bassett,' came an unmistakeably feminine response.

'So tell me, or am I supposed to guess it?' The man was plainly suspicious, as he made no effort to open the door.

'I'm not talking to woodwork,' retorted Angie sharply. 'Surely you big men aren't afraid of a vulnerable and defenceless young female.'

There was brief muttering inside and then two bolts were slammed back and the door swung open. As a heavy storm lamp was thrust forward, the threshold was suddenly flooded with yellowish light. Two men stood in the entrance. The one with the lantern had a Bowie knife in a scabbard strapped to his waist, whilst the other sported an ancient Colt Walker. As their eyes settled on the unexpected visitor, they variously registered a mixture of recognition and interest.

'Well, hey, look who it is,' remarked the lunger with the knife. Neither of Meeker's original assailants had been conscious by the time she had made her entrance in the trading post, but this one remembered her arrival at the Bassett spread as Ray Spence's prisoner. 'You're the little bitch that travels with that gunhand, Rance. Thought Amos and Billy Bob might have done for you by now, *bitch*.'

The other man was slower on the up-take and saw her only as an unexpectedly attractive diversion. Placing the muzzle of his horse pistol against her chest, he remarked, 'Come on in, little lady and welcome. Only be real careful with that carbine. I'd hate to have to pop a cap on you. We've got better plans for you, haven't we, Lee?'

Angie spread her arms slightly, as though in a gesture of supplication. 'Don't either of you want to know what Mister Bassett's message was?'

The two men exchanged baffled glances and it was at that moment that Rance intuitively made his move. Slipping the stubby barrels of his sawn-off under the massive Colt, he heaved it sharply upwards. Its dissolute owner, Chester, jerked back in surprise. In doing so, his trigger finger contracted and there was a tremendous crash. As the heavy ball slammed into the door frame, the accompanying powder flash burst forth and Angie screamed.

Fearing the worst, Rance erupted across the threshold like an avenging angel. Without hesitation, he rammed the gaping muzzles of his shotgun into Chester's torso and squeezed a single trigger. At such point-blank range, the twelve-gauge cartridge literally destroyed him. With his linen shirt on fire, the dead man tumbled back on to the timber floor and lay there twitching slightly.

Befuddled by the blast and surrounded by a cloud of choking, sulphurous smoke, Lee made the mistake of dropping the kerosene lamp and instinctively reaching for his fighting knife. By some miracle, the sturdy lantern landed on its base and remained upright and undamaged. With his ears ringing painfully in the confined space, Rance chose not to detonate the second chamber. Instead, he brutally smashed the butt of his shotgun into Lee's cadaverous features. With a strangled cry, that individual joined his crony on the floor. As the sickly sweet smell of Chester's burning flesh assaulted his nostrils, Rance desperately twisted around to examine Angie.

He had expected the worst and so was almost overwhelmed with relief when he saw that she was unharmed. Black powder residue coated her forehead and her eyebrows had been singed, but she was on her feet and still clutching her Winchester.

'Thank God,' exclaimed Rance,

reaching out to her. 'If anything had happened to you, it would have gone badly for them!'

Chad Seevers, who had stayed by her side, blinked rapidly as he took in the carnage before him. He had experienced violence before, with rustlers and the like, but nothing to compare with this. That and Rance's gallows humour left him suddenly unsure how to proceed. The ranch owner's natural authority seemed to count for nothing in such brutal circumstances.

Satisfied that Angie was unhurt, Rance returned to the two unfortunate Bassett hands. Chester had quite obviously departed his vale of tears, whereas Lee had merely lost a couple of teeth and all his confidence. Glancing quickly around the large room, his assailant called back over his shoulder, 'Chad, you and Angie keep your eyes and guns on the move. We don't know who all else is left around here.' With that, he abruptly turned his attention on to Lee. 'As I recall, you intended using that toad stabber on Wes Meeker, you miserable bull turd.'

Through his mangled lips, Lee desperately tried to get his words out. 'I never meant him no harm, mister. It was Spence who put me up to it!'

He might as well have not wasted the effort. Ignoring his response, Rance barked out, 'Who else is left on this spread?'

'No one. There were just us two. Bassett had business elsewhere.'

His inquisitor peered at him sharply. 'There's a very short list of people that I trust and you're not on it. So I'll ask you again. How many's left hereabouts?' As he spoke, he suddenly surged forward and placed his right boot over Lee's right forearm. Angling down, he forced all his weight on to it, so that the hand was painfully pinned to the floor. With grim intent, Rance pressed the shotgun muzzles on to the outstretched and defenceless palm. 'Think on this before you answer. When I squeeze this trigger, you won't even be able to pick your nose with that knife.'

Lee screamed out in abject terror. 'For pity's sake, mister. I told you the truth.'

Back near the door, Chad Seevers had seen enough. 'Let him go, Toller. We didn't come here for this.'

'Go to hell,' Rance snarled. 'This is all scum bellies like him understand.' With that, his finger began to tighten on the trigger.

As the former lawman well knew, at that moment, Lee would have done anything to avoid losing his extremity and so inevitably he spoke the absolute truth. 'Bassett took everyone 'cept Chester and me. He wants to help Hastings get those broncs saddle-broke and on their way south. They're all expecting a big payday from the army. Honest, mister, there's no one else here. You've got the run of the place!'

Rance stared at him long and hard and then abruptly nodded in apparent satisfaction. Suddenly lulled into a false sense of security, the ranch-hand could never have expected what was to come. Rapidly reversing his big gun, Rance smashed the butt down on to Lee's knife hand with enough force to break bone.

As that man screamed, this time in agony, his tormentor impassively extracted the outsize knife from its scabbard and strode over to the entrance. Sliding the blade behind the door, he exerted all his strength and snapped the Bowie in two.

'You won't need this again,' he laconically remarked. 'And if I was you, I'd get that hand seen to.'

Seevers stared at him with great distaste, whilst Angie remained unhelpfully silent. 'I don't like your methods, Toller.'

'Maybe so, but I'm alive, ain't I?' was the uncompromising response. 'Both of you grab all the oil lamps you can find. We need a proper blaze here. Smoke alone won't be enough.'

As he reloaded the empty chamber of his shotgun, his drooling victim bawled up at him, 'Who the hell are you, anyway, that you'd do this to me?'

Rance regarded him implacably. 'As I keep telling everyone, Angie and I are just passing through. Seems like nobody around here'll believe me!'

It was a short while later when Klee first noticed the strange glow in the night sky off to the west. He was standing out in the open, contentedly smoking his final roll-up of the day and really wished that he hadn't seen it. Reluctantly, he turned to face the barn, owned until recently by Wesley Meeker, and announced, 'You'd better come and take a look at this, boss. Something sure ain't right back at our place!'

Bassett moved surprisingly quickly for such a large man. Barrelling out of their temporary accommodation, he quickly spotted the strange phenomenon. 'For Christ's sake, that's a fire and a big one.' His eyes widened like saucers as he realized its implications. The big house. All his expensive furniture freighted out from the East at horrendous cost. Rational thought was abandoned and he made a knee-jerk decision. 'Klee, get our men saddled up and make it fast.'

That man gazed at his leader in dismay. He was tired and really didn't want to rush off anywhere. 'But Lee and Chester are back there,' he protested.

'They aren't worth a damn,' Bassett responded scathingly. 'Now get moving or you'll be supping from the cup of sorrow!'

That was no idle threat and Klee knew it. Hurrying back into the darkened barn, he noisily rousted out the reluctant Bassett hands and soon the whole bunch was streaming back towards a very uncertain situation.

Nelson Cross rolled on to his side in the hay and looked over at the dark mound that he knew to be Cole Hastings. 'Kind of hard to get any shut-eye around here, what with the noise an' all.'

Hastings grunted non-committedly. He knew there was more to come and besides, the pain from his ruined nose meant that for him *any* sleep was hard to come by.

'I reckon that big-mouthed bastard is just speeding to his death,' continued the black-clad outlaw. 'He can't see beyond that damned mahogany desk of his.'

'And if there is trouble waiting for him,' contributed Hastings at last, 'then dime to a dollar it'll be those cockchafers that have been dogging our trail. So what say we bushwhack the bushwhackers?'

'That does have a nice ring to it,' Cross acknowledged and so it wasn't long before two more riders headed off towards the Bassett ranch. Hastings had wisely decided to let his own men rest and so lessen the chance of mishaps in the dark.

*   *   *

Alone amongst the Bar S ranch-hands, Charlie Peach had experience of brutal bloody violence. Years of fighting the Chiricahua Apaches had taught him the value of a good ambush. The ramrod, Buck Slidell, had reluctantly deferred to the former scout's greater knowledge and allowed himself and the rest of the men to be positioned behind trees or in clumps of vegetation. Even the sound of gunshots from the farmhouse did not distract Charlie. He had already decided that the man called Rance would likely be equal to any opposition found there. Angie's friend had the look of someone who was used to trouble in all its many forms.

As flames began to appear from the house, Charlie called out to the others. 'Remember, boys. Anyone coming out of the darkness is your enemy, so shoot to kill!' With that, he retracted the hammer of his Sharps carbine and made ready. It seemed like old times, with the butt of the powerful weapon tucked into his shoulder. Its rate of fire was less than a lever-action repeater, but it was accurate and hit hard.

For seemingly an age, the men crouched there. The only sound was the crackling of flames as Herb Bassett's prized possessions were voraciously consumed by fire. Charlie knew that even at a distance the waiting men would be partially back-lit, but he was confident that whoever turned up on horseback wouldn't be given the chance to benefit from it. It crossed his mind that neither his boss nor Rance Toller had re-appeared; yet they had to have survived to have started the inferno. Then he made out the sound of thrumming hoofs and life suddenly became very simple: kill or be killed!

As the shod horses rapidly approached, the former Indian fighter could sense exactly how his men were feeling. 'Steady, *compadres*,' he called out softly. 'You just listen out for the sound of my truthful Sharps and then give them hell!'

As the fire really took hold, tongues of flame leapt into the night sky and flickering light spread far beyond the corral and the adjacent buildings. Urged on by their raging leader, the charging horsemen suddenly burst into view. Even as Herb Bassett bellowed out, 'Form a bucket chain from the well, goddamn it,' Charlie Peach drew a fine bead on the nearest rider and fired.

As the potent weapon crashed out, the rest of his men followed suit and a ragged fusillade rattled off. Powder flashes erupted all around, robbing them of any last vestiges of night vision. The initial volley had brought down a number of men and animals, so that screams now mingled with the gunfire. It was all very encouraging and yet Charlie's men were inexperienced at such work. Nervously, they fired as fast as they could work their lever actions. Inevitably, too much of the hot lead flew harmlessly off into the night.

Herb Bassett belatedly realized his mistake and bellowed out at his remaining men to dismount and find cover. The loss of his house was bitterly hard to take, but at last he began to think straight. 'Shoot at the powder flashes,' he commanded. 'Those sons of bitches are going to suffer for this!'

As the Bar S man nearest to Charlie had his jaw shot away, the scout cursed bitterly, before hollering, 'Save your cartridges. Don't shoot unless you've got a sure target and then shift position. Fast.'

*　*　*

Over beyond the burning house, Chad Seevers agitatedly observed the chaotic battle until he could restrain himself no longer. 'I ain't skulking around in the dark like a Dutch gal.' So saying, he leapt to his feet, only to be firmly restrained by a powerful grip.

'Whoever led them into this has got rocks for brains. Stick around and see what occurs,' Rance urged forcefully.

Chad Seevers was a proud man who had had enough of taking a subservient role. Wrenching his arm clear, he barked out, 'Not likely! Those are my men fighting out there.'

Clutching his Winchester, the ranch owner advanced towards his embattled Bar S hands. For a moment, he was fully illuminated by the glare of the blazing building and that was all the time it took. From off to his flank, in the cover of some trees, two shots rang out. A .36-calibre ball struck Seevers in his torso, whilst a shaped bullet ploughed into the soft flesh of his neck. With a strangled cry, the mortally wounded man collapsed to the ground.

Cole Hastings knew all about the

fire-and-move rule. He was shifting position before the smoke had even cleared from his gun muzzle. Sensing that flanking Bassett's assailants might well prove rewarding, he moved swiftly away without even consulting his companion.

Nelson Cross, arrogant and over-confident, chose to wait on events. He wasn't to be disappointed.

'Cover me!' yelled Rance as he leapt forward. Zigzagging from side to side, he fired first one barrel of his sawn-off and then the next.

'How am I supposed to do that if you keep leaping about like a loon?' Angie retorted.

Over in the trees, the black-clad gunfighter suddenly found himself peppered with a wide spread of shot. At least three pieces of lead struck non-vital parts of his body. The little finger of his left hand was almost severed and flesh was gouged out of his chest in two places. Ever calculating and professional, Cross ignored the intense stabbing pains and returned fire. His Colt Navy bucked twice in his hand, but he was up against a moving target and both balls went wide.

Rance reloaded on the move and immediately fired once. His opponent had ducked behind a tree, which saved him from further injury, but put him squarely on the defensive. The shotgun crashed out once more at close range and a tight pattern of shot tore into the trunk.

'That's your two,' snarled Cross triumphantly as his gun hand swung out from cover. The revolver fired, but Rance had already dropped flat. Then Angie finally did as instructed. Rapidly working the lever-action of her carbine, she fired a flurry of shots at the beleaguered shootist. Taking advantage of the backup, Rance quickly reloaded both chambers and then rolled to his left.

'Keep firing, Angie,' he bellowed, before triggering another twelve-gauge cartridge.

Nelson Cross had never before encountered anything like this. As an accomplished *pistolero* he possessed a ruthless finesse, but now he was up against a bludgeon, a brutal slugger who just never knew when to quit. Bullets from the bitch's Winchester kept striking the tree and then that goddamned shot-gun fired again. Lead pellets tore into Cross's partially exposed right leg and suddenly he just couldn't take any more.

Lurching into the open, the wounded gunfighter frantically headed towards Bassett's much reduced force. That man spotted the sudden movement through the smoke-filled gloom and snapped off a well-judged shot. The bullet caught Nelson Cross full on in the chest and he went down as though poleaxed.

Back near the burning ranch house, Angie's attention was taken by a weak cry from the ground nearby. 'For pity's sake, don't let me die alone.'

The mortally wounded Chad Seevers obviously hadn't got long and his pitiful entreaty tugged at her. Suddenly aware that she was dangerously bathed in light, the young woman dropped to her knees. In her time with Rance she had learnt a few things and so took the time to reload her carbine before crawling over to where he lay. Blood glistened on his neck as he desperately reached out to her. She allowed her fingers to intertwine with his and was shocked at the weakness of his grip.

'We could have been something, you and me,' he croaked earnestly. 'If only things had worked out differently.'

Angie knew from hard experience that 'if only' were the two saddest words in any language and so she gazed at him in shocked surprise. It was only now, for the first time, that she realized he must have been harbouring feelings of a romantic nature for her. If such was the case, then what must he have felt when Rance Toller had abruptly reappeared? An uncontrollable tremor surged through his dying body. 'Hold me,' he pleaded and so she did. It was with his head cradled in her arms that he finally passed away.

Rance also had call to minister to the dying, although in a very different way. Keeping low, he warily closed in on Nelson Cross's last position and soon discovered his broken body. Herb Bassett's bullet had struck a vital organ and the black-clad shootist was obviously existing on borrowed time.

'Was it you killed Wes Meeker?' Rance demanded coldly.

Blood frothed over Cross's lips as he gasped out a reply. 'Yes and I enjoyed it. I take pleasure from … killing.' Then he shuddered and his eyes glazed over. 'Just who the hell are you, anyway?' he managed.

If he had expected a reply, then he was to be sadly disappointed, because his grim assailant just gazed down at him bleakly. Rance was heartily sick of the same damn fool question and the man expiring before him certainly didn't deserve any kind of closure.

Cole Hastings appeared out of the murk like a wraith. Herb Bassett jerked in surprise as he suddenly found the outlaw's hard eyes fixed on him. 'You right sure which side you're on, Herb?' he snarled. 'That last shot put Cross down for keeps.'

Recovering his composure, Bassett retorted, 'He came at me unawares and besides, he was a loose cannon. He went beyond his orders and tried to rob me of my share in something.'

With gunfire continuing in front of them and now a shotgun crashing out on their flank, it was obviously time to retreat, but Hasting's wasn't finished. 'Maybe he did and maybe he didn't. Just don't go misremembering where we stand, is all. If I have to come at you, you won't get any warning. You'll just be dead. Savvy?'

Even in the poor light, Bassett couldn't disguise the sick look that came to his face. 'OK, OK. Let's just get the hell out of here while we can,' he replied testily. 'Something tells me this ain't over yet.'

13

'Well that's it then,' commented Buck Slidell glumly. 'It's all over.'

'Like hell, it is!' cried Angie sharply. To Rance's great surprise, she stormed over to the ramrod and glared up at him. 'You've still got a job to do!'

The Bar S's longest serving employee stared at her in amazement and then glanced around at the other survivors for support. They in turn, confused at the turn of events, found it hard to meet his eyes. Three of their number were out of the fight; two dead and one in a pain-filled stupor with half of his face blown away. The rest of them felt strangely lost. Numbed by the violence and unaccountably thirsty, they had lost their leader and Buck was no substitute. Charlie Peach had the makings, but he didn't consider it to be his place to take the lead. And besides, take the lead to do what?

Angie gazed around at them all in the waning light of the fire. Still deeply moved by Seevers' surprise disclosure, she was in no doubt about what needed to be done. 'You sorry sons of bitches. Don't you pay this fella no heed. You had a good man there in Chad Seevers and you owe it to him to finish the job.'

Rance was puzzled by her sudden fervour, but smiled at the young woman proudly as he moved over to join her. Of all of them, he was most qualified for the task ahead and as was his nature he didn't waste any time on soft talk. 'And *finish* the job is exactly what we are *all* going to do,' he stated firmly. 'Because I ain't going to let you guys just slope off and become a bunch of quitters. Charlie, I reckon if you got yourself situated on the ridge overlooking Meeker's spread with that truthful Sharps, you could make things very warm for those varmints.'

With a hierarchy apparently re-established, the scout decided that he definitely liked the idea. 'Oh, I can make them hop and squeal, all right,' he affirmed. 'I'll take one man with a repeater, in case they try to rush me.'

The only dissenting voice was that of the ramrod, who belatedly resented his loss of authority. 'Just what is your aim, mister?' he rasped.

Rance settled his hard eyes on him. 'You remember what Grant did to Lee outside Petersburg in the late conflict?'

Buck was completely stumped at the apparently irrelevant reference, but Rance carried on anyway. 'His army hit the Confederates again and again. He never let up and he never gave Lee any respite. Well that's what we're going to do to those goddamned rustlers over yonder. Bassett's lost his house and next it'll be his life.' Clapping his hands vigorously, he urged, 'So let's be about it!'

The men glanced sheepishly at Angie, before slowly nodding their assent. It occurred to them that whoever was waiting over at Meeker's couldn't possibly be any tougher than the two people standing before them.

The first long-range killing took place just as the new day arrived with enough light to make gunplay possible. The victim was one of Hastings' crew, who had not been part of the night's violence. As he unwisely made his way towards the water pump, a large calibre bullet brutally lifted off the top of his head. He was dead before the powder smoke had cleared away up on the ridge. By the time the shocked rustlers opened up with their own weapons, Charlie had already shifted position.

Another man ran for the corral to get a better angle and the powerful rifle fired again. He slewed sideways with a bullet in his right lung and coughed blood on to the hard earth. Up on the ridge, Charlie grunted in satisfaction and moved again.

'Keep under cover, goddamn it,' bellowed Hastings angrily. 'Or that poxy buffalo gun'll open us all up.'

Herb Bassett, sleepless and smarting from the night's reverses, was almost beside himself with rage. 'Those ass boils are using the ridge,' he snarled before

226

declaring petulantly. 'That's *my* ridge!'

Hastings glared at him impatiently. 'Well it's their ridge now and the only way we'll get them off it is to flank them.'

Jake Ridgeway, still smarting from his bruising encounter with Hastings, offered a doom-laden prophesy. 'This is all going to go sour. I can feel it in my bones, Cole. We'd do well to pull out while we can and you'd do well to mark my words.'

The gang leader's response was uncompromising. 'I'll *mark* your bleeding face if you don't do what I say!' He was just about to issue instructions for an assault on the ridge, when one of his gang yelled a warning.

'There's movement over near the river, Cole.'

That man angrily twisted around. 'Sweet Jesus, what now?'

★   ★   ★

The huge herd had drunk its fill and was contentedly grazing on the lush grass along the banks of the Green River. No guard had been posted, as it was considered unlikely that anyone would have the *cojones* to rustle from the rustlers and besides, they'd had other things on their minds. Rance, Buck and Angie, along with the seven remaining Bar S hands, were spread out to the south of the stolen horses. Off in the distance, Wesley Meeker's barn was clearly visible.

'You ever been in a stampede?' Rance called over to the young woman sitting her horse nearest to him.

Angie was scared, but doing her level best to hide it. 'Only every time I enter a saloon,' she archly replied.

'Good answer. I suppose there's no point in asking you to stay behind.'

'None whatsoever!'

'That's what I figured.' Turning to the others, he raised his voice and said, 'This herd's going to take some shifting. Fire into the ground, real close and try to steer them straight at the barn.'

The men all nodded grimly and suddenly there was nothing left to say. Cocking his shotgun, Rance peered down the extended line and nodded. A ragged volley crashed out and an assortment of projectiles smacked in to the ground near the peacefully grazing animals. This, along with the muzzle flashes and acrid smoke, had an awesome effect. Those terrified horses nearest the discharge instinctively took flight in the opposite direction. This took them careering into their neighbours, who in turn fled north creating a knock-on effect as they went. With their tormentors whooping and firing behind them, the whole herd was soon a panic-stricken heaving mass pounding across the grassland.

'Don't let them turn,' yelled Rance as he moved to intercept some strays.

With the river on their right, Seevers' men only had one flank to watch and so it proved a relatively easy task to keep the animals on track. Her heart thumping with excitement, Angie actually forgot the danger as she found herself yelling uninhibitedly along with the others. Taking part in a stampede was turning out to be the most fun that she had had in ages and so it slipped her mind that there was a serious purpose behind it.

The ground flashed by beneath them and soon the lead animals were approaching the mixed collection of intact and burnt-out buildings that the late Wesley Meeker had once called home. Up on the ridge, Charlie Peach commented to his awestruck companion, 'Holy shit, will you look at that. They're moving full chisel. Jesus Christ his self couldn't stop that lot!'

That blasphemous opinion was shared by both Cole Hastings and Herb Bassett. Pinned under cover by the deadly Sharps, their options had rapidly become very limited.

'Drop some of the leaders,' yelled Ridgeway hopefully. 'It might turn them.'

'Like hell you will,' snarled Hastings as he pushed the other man's rifle aside. 'That's cash money on the hoof. Every man into the loft. We'll wait them out!'

The others didn't need telling twice. As they leapt up the wooden ladders, the frightened men just prayed that

Meeker's barn was as strong as it looked. No animal will willingly collide with a solid object, but by this time the herd's momentum was unstoppable. From behind the seething multitude, gunshots were clearly audible.

With their covering fire no longer needed, Charlie and his companion mounted up and headed down the steep slope. Any conflict was likely to be at close range from now on and they wanted to be in on it.

With the frightened herd racing flat out, the climax to the stampede came very quickly. Suddenly aware of the large building ahead, the lead animals desperately tried to move aside, but they were hemmed in from the sides and propelled by the sheer weight of horseflesh. Nothing could prevent the gruesome pile-up. With a tremendous smash that Rance and his companions could hear at the rear, even over the noise of pounding hoofs, the doomed leaders surged into the barn and hit the rear wall.

Under such pressure the planking

gave way, but not before many animals had tripped and been crushed by those following. With screams that were almost human, the poor beasts piled up underneath the hayloft.

'Sounds like plenty ain't going to be fit for the army after all,' commented Ridgeway slyly. 'Maybe we should have tried my way....'

Ignoring him, Hastings lay down on the fresh hay and waited impatiently for the mad rush to subside. Even though the main support timbers had trembled under the shock, the barn had survived the initial impact, as had all the rustlers. However, there was no denying that they were now trapped inside with all freedom of movement gone.

For what seemed like an age, the panic-stricken horses flowed through the structure. It vibrated as though alive and choking dust filled the atmosphere. Then, with Rance and the others having ceased fire and now holding back, the pressure from behind gradually eased. Some of the animals began to avoid the barn altogether and at last those running through it began to peter out.

Pointing at two ranch-hands, Rance ordered, 'Get round the back and shoot anything on two legs that shows itself, you hear?'

The two men obeyed readily enough, but Buck Slidell wasn't at all happy. 'What gives you the right to give instructions to my men, mister?'

Rance was in no mood to offer considerations. 'Right now they're not your men. They're mine until I've finished with them. Savvy?'

The ramrod blanched, but held his tongue. There was something about the shotgun-toting stranger that gave him pause and besides, that man wasn't even looking at him any more. Dismounting, Rance nodded amiably at Charlie Peach as he approached. 'You did good on the ridge, fella.'

That man chuckled and patted his weapon. 'Windage and elevation. That's all you need to watch with one of these beauties.'

Rance smiled appreciatively and then addressed the whole group. 'Now if anybody holding a shooting iron shows themselves from that barn, make them regret it.'

The ten of them spread out and waited for the remaining wild horses to clear out of the way. The herd was now scattered like leaves in the wind, but it had served its purpose and Rance was now eager to proceed. 'You in the barn,' he yelled, 'throw your firearms on the ground and come out with your hands held high, or I'll finish what you started and set this place to burning.'

Not for the first time, Angie looked at him askance. 'Why is it that you want to torch every building you come across?'

Rance regarded her fondly. 'Folks ought to make them out of something else if they don't want them burned to the ground.'

Up in the hayloft, Cole Hastings and Herb Bassett regarded each other with considerably less warmth. 'That's the son of a bitch that gave us a bloody nose at the old cabin,' Hastings stated irately. 'Your man Spence should have finished the job properly.' Without awaiting a response, he began to smash a loophole through the planking with the butt of his rifle.

Outside, everyone dropped flat and unleashed a volley at the first floor. Woodchips flew off, but it seemed unlikely that any lead actually penetrated the solid timber.

'That place is built like a fort,' remarked the former army scout.

Rance had no doubt what needed to be done. 'Bundle up some hay and sticks,' he called over to the nearest of Seevers' men. 'I'll invest one of my Lucifers.'

Angie crawled over to him and grabbed his hand. 'There's wounded animals in there. I'll not let you burn them alive. It's not right and it's not Christian!'

Rance sighed and inspected her strained but still lovely features closely. He could see that she was deadly serious. 'That conscience of yourn will get you into trouble one of these days,' he responded softly. Then, much louder, he called out, 'Charlie, you reckon you might could be able to pick off the injured beasts in there? This young lady suffers from finer feelings.'

'Oh sure. No problem at all,' came the calm reply. 'And killing animals never bothered me any. You slay his pony, it makes an Apache warrior more apt to be reasonable.' So saying, he lowered his line of sight and took careful aim. As each measured shot rang out, a suffering creature was put out of its misery, but up in the loft there was confusion.

'What in tarnation is that buffalo gun shooting at?' demanded Herb Bassett. 'Because it sure as hell isn't us.'

Hastings cautiously peered over the edge of the floor boarding. 'Someone out there's got scruples, that's what,' he responded. 'They don't mind us frying, but not some dumb animal.' Getting quickly to his feet, he rounded on Bassett. 'Which means that those sons of bitches ain't bluffing. We've got to get out of here while we can.'

For all his bluster, Bassett was no fool. 'And we still outnumber them. They can't cover all four sides at once. Let's smash our way out and scatter. That way we get another chance at the herd.'

Outside, Rance cocked his head to one side as he pondered the sudden frantic activity. 'They're making a break for it. We've got to move fast.' Withdrawing a precious Lucifer from an empty cartridge case sealed with wax, he soon had the dry makings burning. 'Cover me,' he demanded and then hefting the blazing fascine, he sprinted for the barn.

One rifle sounded off at him, but the marksman was unable to depress his weapon enough in the loophole and it was immediately answered by a fusillade. Breathlessly, Rance slammed up against the wall next to the entrance and heaved the flaming torch into the interior. The bone-dry hay strewn about the floor set alight instantly and he grunted with satisfaction. The fire-starter was about to retrace his steps, but then had second thoughts and instead drew and cocked his Remington. The sudden inferno was bound to bring a reaction and as it happened, he didn't have long to wait.

As flames rapidly spread to the lower walls, one of Bassett's men, already rattled from the night before, abruptly decided that the barn had lost its charms. 'The hell with this,' he howled. 'We're all dead for sure up here.' With that, he dashed for the ladder.

His fear was infectious and the rest of the rancher's men immediately followed him. Their boss angrily trained his rifle on to them, but Hastings snapped out, 'Let the curs go. They'll create a diversion. We can use it.'

With the half dozen fugitives swarming down the steps, he urged his own men to break through the back and side walls. As a man-size hole was smashed through the back of the barn, the two men stationed there by Rance fired up at the opening. They weren't particularly good shots, but their mere presence could well stop the escape in its tracks.

At the front entrance, Rance heard boots thumping on wooden steps as Bassett's men fled the loft. It sounded like there were plenty of them. After signalling back to the others that trouble was coming, he boldly stepped out from cover with his revolver level and steady. Secure in the knowledge that he wasn't visible from the loft, he called out, 'Drop those fire sticks, boys, or get to dying!'

Five of the outlaws were uncertainly milling around near a pile of burning hay, trying to decide which way to run. A sixth was still clinging to the ladder. Of the five, three held Winchesters and two toted revolvers. To a man, they registered horrified surprised at the sudden challenge and froze rigid.

Rance knew that that was the tipping point and that matters could easily go either way. 'You heard me,' he snarled. 'Drop those smoke wagons.'

Up in the loft, Cole Hastings shouldered his man out of the way at the back wall and took swift but steady aim through the newly battered opening.

To those watching, it seemed as though he didn't even have to think about it. The gunfighter just squeezed off a shot, switched targets and fired again. Neither smoke nor recoil affected the bloody outcome. Both Bar S trail-hands took a lethal bullet and tumbled to the ground, twitching in their death throes. The way was open for a swift retreat.

Ironically, it was those two shots that broke the brief deadlock downstairs. The sixth man was still immobile on the ladder, but the one on the far left was shocked into action by the sharp reports. He brandished a Schofield revolver and was suddenly in an itching hurry to use it.

'Aw shit,' murmured Rance unhappily as he aimed and fired. The bullet struck the man square in his chest and his gun hand suddenly sagged uncontrollably, as though dragged down by a great weight. He was out of the fight, but now everyone else apparently wanted a piece of it. From then on Rance acted purely on instinct, drawing on years of experience as a lawman. By taking into account the weapons that his opponents carried and the positions that they adopted, he was able to prioritize his firing order.

Only one other man held a revolver and so that marked him out as the next victim. Rapidly cocking and firing, Rance again aimed at the torso, that being the largest target by far. This time his victim let loose a great scream as the bullet smashed through ribs and punctured a lung. Coughing blood, he staggered back, effectively out of action. As powder smoke mingled with wood smoke, Rance calmly held his ground and fired yet again. This time the selected outlaw had just about got his Winchester up level and so lost out by only a tiny margin. The bullet hit him on the move and shattered his right arm at the elbow. Howling in agony, he dropped his rifle and stumbled sideways, straight into the path of his two companions, who in turn fell back towards the ladder.

Rance had been about to tackle them, but instead stepped forward into the barn and targeted the individual on the steps. That man had been on the point of jumping to the ground, but finding his way barred he twisted awkwardly so as to get a shot. His implacable foe fired for the fourth time and brought him crashing down the ladder on to his cronies. With two chambers still remaining, Rance had effectively routed the whole bunch, but unfortunately for him he was now visible from the hayloft.

Herb Bassett was about to flee the premises, but took the time to snap off a hasty shot at the man who had destroyed his prized house. The bullet punched into Rance's left shoulder and caused him to spin around so that he was no longer facing into the barn. Behind him, one of the two cowboys finally got himself situated and lined his Winchester up on Rance's helpless form.

'This is for all those you've killed, you heartless son of a bitch!'

14

Angie Sutter watched her lover collapse to the ground and cried out in disbelief. Instinctively, she broke into a run and so was unprepared to intervene when the ranch-hand suddenly appeared with his rifle aimed directly at Rance. Desperately, the young woman ground to a halt and raised her weapon, but she knew in her heart that she was both out of position and out of time.

Charlie Peach wanted to bawl at her to get out of the way. With her body partially obstructing his view it was a very tight shot, but he kept cool and saved his breath. Taking careful aim, he squeezed the twin triggers just as his target uttered the fateful words to Rance. Angie actually felt the blast of pressure as the heavy bullet passed her, prior to striking the cowboy right between his eyes and removing the back of his head.

In spite of the awesome throbbing in his shoulder, Rance had retained his grip on the Remington and so rolled over to face the sole remaining adversary. That man's eyes bugged out as the grim reality of his situation struck him. Dropping his rifle, he cried out, 'Sweet Jesus, mister. Don't shoot!'

With his thoughts dominated by pain, Rance's finger tightened on the trigger. His eyes held a lethal intent that provided his victim with absolutely no hope. As he stared death in the face, that man was suddenly aware of a rush of warm liquid down his left leg and he burst into tears. Something about the pathetic sight penetrated Rance's murderous resolve and brought him to his senses. Uttering a great sigh, he allowed the tension in his trigger finger to ease.

And then in a flash, Angie was upon him. 'You madman. I thought you was kilt for sure. Don't you ever do that again!' With the inferno all the while developing around them, she pointed her Winchester at the surviving cowboy. 'Get rid of that belt gun, you son of a bitch and then hightail it before I shoot you myself.'

As the man hastened to comply, Rance helpfully added his own comment, 'If I ever see you again, I'll kill you.'

In her relief at his survival, Angie was unexpectedly overcome by a fit of giggles. 'Do you think he got the message? I mean, just look at him run,' she gasped.

Rance glanced unsympathetically at the fleeing cowboy. The sudden movement provoked a grunt of discomfort and abruptly the light-hearted moment was over.

'Let me see your shoulder,' Angie demanded, but before she could do anything, Charlie and the others were upon them.

'Hot dang. I ain't never seen the like before,' pronounced the scout jubilantly. 'You took on six of the dogs and got off with a flesh wound. It is just a flesh wound, isn't it?' he queried hopefully.

Angie began to tug at his coat, until Rance decided that enough was enough. Shaking her off, he stated, 'Whatever it is, it can wait. Those pus weasels got out through the back wall, which means we've probably got two dead round there and you've got scores to settle. Remember what I said about Grant and Lee? We've got to keep hitting them before they get chance to regroup. Now, while they're all afoot.' As the remnants of Seevers' men nodded agreement, he called out, 'Now get my damned horse over here!'

As Buck and the others rounded up the animals, Charlie helped Rance to his feet so that they could get away from the searing heat. With Angie having reloaded his revolver, they then both helped to heave the wounded man into his saddle. Rance swayed slightly as he battled with shock, but it wasn't the first time that he'd been shot. 'Let's ride,' he commanded through gritted teeth and then they were off.

Charging around to the rear of the blazing barn, they soon spotted the escaping rustlers. Wearing riding boots and burdened with firearms, those men were making a very poor job of running.

'Herd them towards the river,'

suggested Charlie. 'It's running too high for them to wade across.'

'Sounds good,' returned Rance as he reeled slightly in the saddle. His left arm and shoulder were aching abominably and he was beginning to feel faint. 'Take the lead,' he added.

Angie watched him closely. The young woman knew he had to be suffering to utter such words and urged her mount protectively closer. And so it was that the eight riders swept around the left flank of the fleeing outlaws, firing mainly for effect as they went.

$$\star \quad \star \quad \star$$

After so much bloodletting, Bassett and Hastings had about a dozen men left between them and panic was beginning to affect some of them. They mostly lived their lives in the saddle and so were ill at ease on foot. As their fast moving pursuers closed in, they found themselves on bottomland, being forced back towards the Green River. Panting heavily, Jake

Ridgeway bellowed out in frustration, 'This won't answer. They'll run us into the river and then just pick us off.' Then his true fear emerged. '*And I can't swim!*'

Cole Hastings was mighty tired of his subordinate's bellyaching. 'Lord sakes. You don't hush up, I'll shoot you myself. Nobody's going swimming. Just get down behind the river-bank. We'll use it to fort up.' As he ran towards the water, he snatched a glance at Bassett and in spite of the parlous circumstances, couldn't resist a malicious smile. The big man normally had plenty to say, but hoofing it across country had left him blown and sweating like the pig that he was.

With their chests heaving, the desperate men finally reached the river and gratefully flung themselves down the bank. All of them would gladly have slaked their thirst, but there just wasn't time. Keeping low, they thrust their weapons over the top. Even the most timid of them now recognized that the situation was suddenly reversed and that it was the pursuing *cavalry* that was at a big disadvantage.

'Hold your fire,' bellowed Hastings. 'Let them get in close so we can bleed them good!'

But then a strange thing happened. The pursuing riders reined in beyond accurate rifle range and just sat there.

★ ★ ★

Rance was sweating heavily and his whole body felt greasy, but he had warded off the light-headedness that had threatened to overwhelm him and still possessed all his faculties. He nodded grimly, as though in agreement with himself and then called over to Charlie Peach. 'A man on their flank with a Sharps could play havoc, don't you reckon?'

'Damn right,' came the reply. 'And I'm that man.' Without more ado, he headed off at a forty-five degree angle and soon reached the river a few hundred yards away from Hastings' crew. With his horse ground-tethered, Charlie unsheathed his buffalo gun and dropped down flat.

Raising the ladder sight, he took careful aim and fired. The cloud of acrid smoke temporarily obscured his view, but that didn't matter. His target had been static and he never missed a shot like that.

Jake Ridgeway never did learn to swim. The .52-calibre bullet hit him in the side of his head and exited out the far side in a mess of blood and bone. His lifeless body fell back down the bank and ended up partially submerged in the Green River.

'Goddamn, but those Sharps make a mess,' muttered Klee dolefully. He was Herb Bassett's sole remaining employee and was beginning to wish that he'd remained in Robbers' Roost.

'That's the first time I've seen Jake take a bath,' Hastings remarked with a notable lack of sympathy. 'Stop crying over him and get some fire down on that bastard sharpshooter.'

Those men with rifles sent a torrent of hot lead up the river-bank, but every bullet fell short and merely kicked up earth. Then Charlie took another well-considered shot and one more of Hastings' rustlers tumbled into the river. More blood flowed into the water, prompting Bassett to make a singularly ill-judged comment. 'They're going to have to rename this river soon.'

In desperation, every man now began scooping shallow trenches out of the river-bank with their bare hands. Anything to escape from the terrifyingly accurate marksman. Such was their frenzy that they actually forgot about that individual's companions who were now about to enter the fray.

As Rance saw that their moment had come, fresh energy surged through his battered body. The final reckoning had arrived and he relished the prospect. He was so fired up that he didn't even make a pointless attempt at keeping Angie out of harm's way. Glancing at the others, he instructed, 'Don't open fire until you see a target and don't show any pity. Those sons of bitches still outnumber us.' With that, he spurred his animal forward and took off towards the river at full pelt.

Charlie Peach's flanking fire was so effective that the seven riders crossed the open ground without a shot being triggered at them. It wasn't until they reached the river-bank that the outlaws became aware of the imminent threat and by then it was too late.

'Powder burn them!' snarled Rance as he aimed his sawn-off down at what was quite obviously the largest target.

At that very instant Cole Hastings, recognizing the voice if not the figure above them, instinctively fired up at Rance's horse. The animal staggered under the impact, which in turn caused its rider to squeeze both triggers at once. Herb Bassett was struck an overwhelmingly devastating blow by the contents of both loads. He died an instant and gory death; he would never see his strong-willed daughters again. As though fated by his recent remark, his blood trickled down into the Green River.

Although not experienced gunhands, the Bar S men were out for revenge and so poured a withering fire down on the rustlers. At such close quarters, accuracy counted for little; so great a quantity of hot lead could not fail to take its toll. In ones and twos, Hastings' followers tumbled back into the river. Some died of gunshot wounds, whilst others slid helplessly under the surface and drowned silently in the depths. For Klee, the old-timer, it was all too much. He simply let his six-gun fall to the ground and waited patiently for the killing to finish.

With his horse dying beneath him, Rance had only just managed to jump clear. He fell heavily and moaned in agony as his left arm jarred under the impact. A few feet away, Cole Hastings again heard the muted boom of the cursed Sharps and yet another of his men collapsed in the mud. He had the wit to realize that the game was up, but if he were going to die he would at least take one particular individual with him, namely, the man responsible for the per-manent disfigurement of his features.

Scaling the embankment at a run, the gunfighter gut shot the nearest Bar S man and then discovered that he was directly facing his nemesis. And with great satisfaction he found that Rance was temporarily incapable of defending himself.

'Seems to me you spend a lot of time skulking behind dead animals,' remarked Hastings spitefully as he lined up a head shot.

His fall had left Rance lying on his good arm and so all he could do was awkwardly crane his neck to look up at the man who fully intended to kill him. Yet even in such a dire situation, he couldn't resist replying with a jibe. 'You don't look so good. Cut yourself shaving?'

Hastings' lips compressed into a tight line and his eyes displayed pure hatred as his finger compressed on the trigger. The first bullet struck him in his left shoulder, causing him to pivot slightly. Unbelievably, his own projectile soared harmlessly off into the flawless blue sky. The next bullet slammed into his right breast. As he staggered back, the shootist desperately tried to focus on his assailant.

'You!' he cried out hoarsely. 'How can it be?'

Angie levered up another cartridge from the cylindrical magazine. 'You should have aimed at me rather than my horse, mister,' she responded bitterly. 'Now drop that gun or I'll finish it.'

With blood pouring from two wounds, Cole Hastings appeared to be done in, but his iron determination just wouldn't leave him. Beads of sweat coated his forehead and seeped into the band of his Confederate slouch hat as he desperately tried to raise his revolver.

'Again, Angie,' Rance cried out. 'Again!'

The young woman aimed her Winchester directly at Hastings' loathsome features, but some female instinct prevented her from taking the kill shot. A ghastly, malevolent smile formed on the outlaw's face as he recognized her weakness. With an almost superhuman effort, he levelled his piece ready yet again to take a human life.

Rance frantically rolled over to free up his good arm, but even as he did so he knew that he had run right out of time. Then, as though in a dream, Angie stared in horrified surprise as Hastings' head abruptly exploded like a ripe melon. As the almost headless corpse toppled to the ground, Rance uttered a great sigh of relief. Knowing full well that only an unusually large bullet could have done such damage, he bellowed out with wild exuberance, 'Well, hurrah for the man with the Sharps!'

15

It was a full twenty-four hours later before anyone got around to considering what the next move should be. With the sole exception of Klee, all the outlaws had perished. Some lay broken and bloodied on the river-bank, whilst others had received a watery grave. At Rance's request, the ruined body of Cole Hastings had been pitched unceremoniously into the river. With only one more fatality amongst the Bar S men, the brief conflict had been amazingly one-sided, but that couldn't alter the fact that there were now only five men left to return to Wyoming.

Not for the first time in his life, Rance had been very lucky. Herb Bassett's bullet had just missed bone and the wound appeared to be clean and unlikely to infect. Since the privy was the only Meeker structure still remaining with a roof on it, Rance lay out in the open as he listened to the men discuss their immediate future.

Unsurprisingly, Buck Slidell was for rounding up the nearest horses and heading back to resume bunkhouse living, albeit under a new owner if any of Chad Seevers kin could be found. 'They'll run themselves out and then drift back to the river,' he predicted knowledgably. 'There'll be a few with necks snapped and legs broke, but it should be easy enough to get a couple of hundred together.'

Rance had heard enough of what he considered to be negative talk. 'There is another option that you probably haven't considered.'

All of the men waited expectantly. They had seen enough of Rance Toller to know that his words carried weight.

'Why not round up the whole herd and do what those murdering bastards had intended. Drive them all down to Arizona and sell them to the army. That way you'll make a tidy profit for your trouble and if any of the original owners do get to hear about it and come looking for trouble, then you just reimburse them.'

Charlie Peach laughed out loud at the audacity of the plan. 'Do "reimburse" mean what I think it do?' he asked Buck.

'It do,' that man responded glumly. He sensed, yet again that he was losing control over his own men.

'Hot dang,' cried Charlie. 'I've never had money to just hand out before. Count me in, mister.'

Buck tried another tack. 'But we haven't got the men to control all those animals,' he protested.

Rance carefully got to his feet. Sensing that their own future was about to be affected, Angie moved over to join him. 'Angie and I were headed for Tombstone anyway. For equal shares, we'll join in as trail-hands.' Then he looked over at the forlorn figure of Klee. That man had been disarmed, but with nowhere to run to, he had remained disconsolately around the camp.

'I don't reckon you're any kind of threat. How's about getting back on wages?'

Klee perked up immediately. 'Sounds

fine to me.' Then, lowering his voice, he muttered, 'Never did take to them murdering trash anyhow.'

And so it was decided. With the former army scout to guide them, the eight survivors would head south. But first they would rest up for a while as the scattered herd gradually returned to water.

Rance and Angie were enjoying their first tranquil moment for many a day. They were standing arm in arm by the Green River, well away from the carnage of the previous day. With the evening well advanced, the sun merely provided gentle warmth rather than intense heat and cast long shadows on to the water.

'So, how do you feel about changing from homesteader to trail-hand?' he mischievously inquired.

Angie chose to evade that question and instead replied in all sincerity. 'I think that the next time we come to some trading post on the Outlaw Trail, we should just go right on by.'

We do hope that you have enjoyed
reading this large print book.

Did you know that all of our titles
are available for purchase?

We publish a wide range of high
quality large print books including:
Romances, Mysteries, Classics
General Fiction
Non Fiction and Westerns

Special interest titles available in
large print are:
The Little Oxford Dictionary
Music Book, Song Book
Hymn Book, Service Book

Also available from us courtesy of
Oxford University Press:
Young Readers' Dictionary
(large print edition)
Young Readers' Thesaurus
(large print edition)

For further information or a free
brochure, please contact us at:
Ulverscroft Large Print Books Ltd.,
The Green, Bradgate Road, Anstey,
Leicester, LE7 7FU, England.
Tel: (00 44) **0116 236 4325**
Fax: (00 44) **0116 234 0205**

DEATH MOUNTAIN

Dale Brandon

After the brutal murder of their employer, Matt Stone and Spider McCaw are determined to track down the culprits. Their search leads them to an outlaw hideout — in the area known as Death Mountain, because nobody attempting to pass has ever come back. The two friends must contend with not only the perilous mountain heights, but also a terrifying menace in a narrow canyon. Can they survive the treacherous journey and bring the killers to justice?

THE SECRET OF THE SILVER STAR

Amos Carr

Outlaw Vince Lange hides a deadly secret: he is really Deputy Marshal Charlie Dane, working undercover to bring down the Carlin gang. When a heavy snowstorm traps the bandits in their hideout, life becomes even more difficult for Dane when Frank Carlin sends him and another outlaw to fetch supplies — but only Dane returns, leaving three bodies and a burned-out ranch behind. Deciding to split the gang and head for the nearest town, Carlin gives Dane a terrible task to complete . . .

RANGE BOSS

Jack Edwardes

The once-prosperous Bar Circle spread has been going downhill since its former owner was found dead in a saloon girl's bed, leaving behind debt and unhappy ranch-hands who talk of quitting. Cattle have been taken by rustlers, and the new owner is struggling to defend the place. Hearing of the ranch's plight and spying the chance to make a quick buck, men are circling like coyotes, ready to kill anyone who stands in their way . . .

JEFFERSON'S SADDLE

Will DuRey

When Charlie Jefferson arrives in the Texas town of Mortimer, left for dead after a brutal ambush and robbery, he is intent on finding the man who did this to him. But he is unwittingly drawn into a plot involving the town council. For, en route to Mortimer from the wasteland where he was left to perish, Jefferson stumbled across a dying Texas Ranger. And by showing mercy to the man, he may have sealed his own fate . . .

RECKONING AT EL DORADO

Scott Connor

When Buster McCloud is accused of killing Aaron Knight and Salvadora Somoza, Marshal Lincoln Hawk wastes no time in arresting him. McCloud confesses to killing Aaron, but swears he never hurt Somoza. Hawk's investigation concludes that she is still alive — and she's not the only woman to have gone missing recently. With all the evidence pointing to ruthless gold prospector Domingo Villaruel, Lincoln must travel into the very heart of the man's empire to uncover the truth.